THE SEXY PART

KYLIE GILMORE

The Sexy Part: © 2023 by Kylie Gilmore

Cover design by: Sweet 'N Spicy Designs

Published by: Extra Fancy Books

ISBN-13: 978-1-64658-129-0

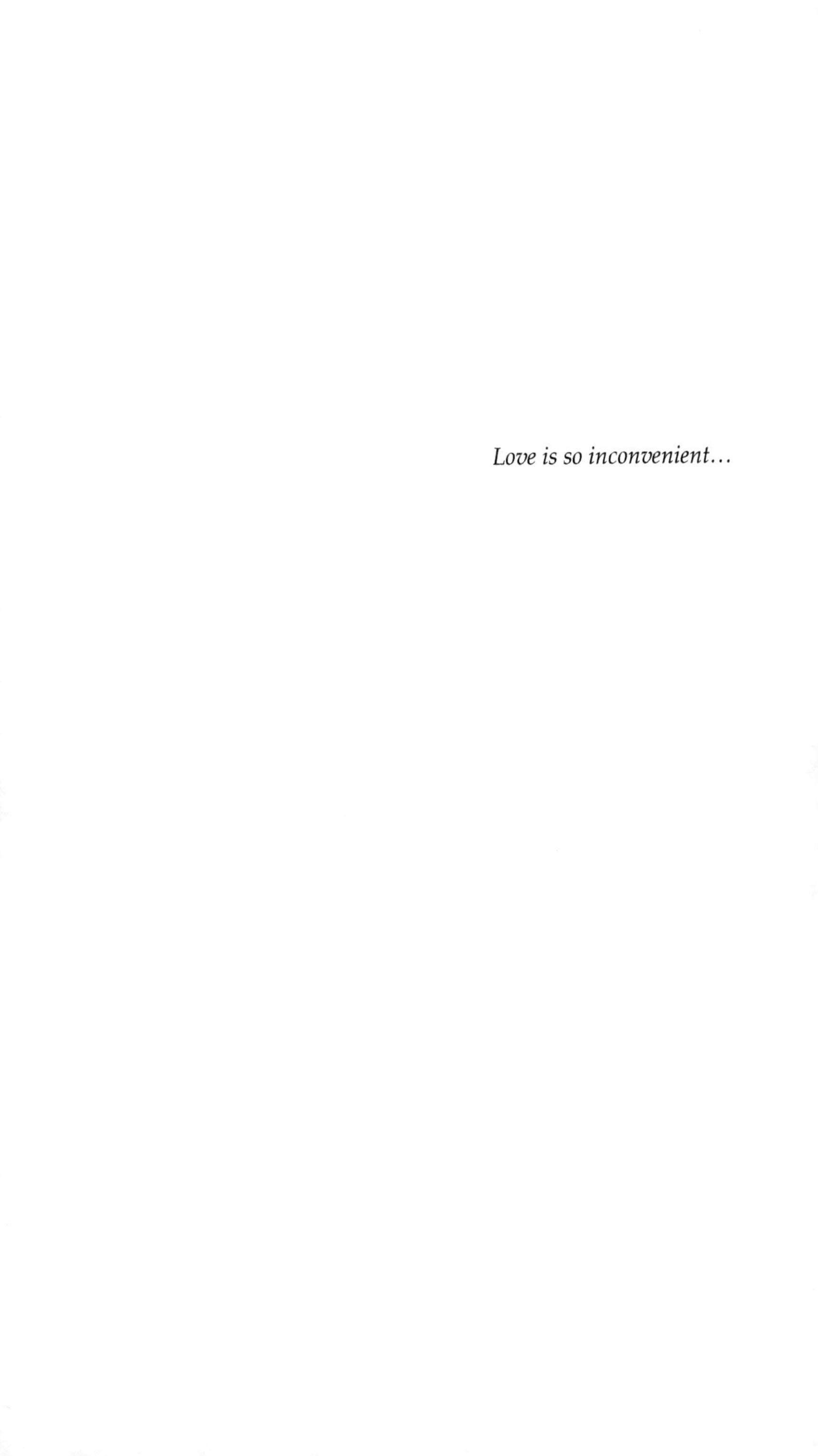

Love is so inconvenient…

1

———

Rowan

I shove the wedding veil out of my face as I march from the scene of the crime, aka my wedding. How could he do this to me? And then I have to find out from *her*? No. Just no. *Burn in hell, Dave.*

I cross the street, heading for the Happy Endings bar and restaurant, where my wedding planner dashed off to give a quick congratulations at some family event. I didn't catch all the details, as I was too busy getting ready for what was *supposed* to be the happiest day of my life. *Grr...*

I glare at the cheerful Happy Endings sign over the front door. This bar may be the only happy ending in my life for a very long time. I yank open the door and step inside. There's a restaurant area to my right, where a huge crowd of people seem to be having the time of their lives. Straight ahead is a dark cherrywood bar. That bar is my second stop. I scan the crowd for the long strawberry-blond hair of my wedding planner, Hailey Campbell.

She hurries toward me, her heels clicking on the tile. Guess I'm easy to find standing here in my wedding gown.

I yank the veil off my head, sending bobby pins flying. "He jilted me! Just up and left! And I had to find out from his ex-girlfriend, who I never wanted at the wedding anyway!"

Hailey's eyes go wide. "Did he leave with her?"

"No." My voice chokes. "She was just the smug messenger."

Hailey's sympathetic look takes me from furious to devastated in a hot second. My lower lip trembles. "Oh, Rowan, I'm—"

I burst into tears.

She hugs me. "I'm so sorry."

I hang on to her for dear life, both surprised and relieved by the hug. After all, we have a professional relationship.

I pull away and sniffle. "I even invited my father, who I haven't seen in three years. This is so humiliating." My older brother—the golden one—showed up too. Everyone's still across the street at the wedding venue, a historic mansion called Ludbury House. I can't face them with the horrible news yet.

Hailey pats my back. "I know. Come with me. We'll get you some water." She guides me toward the bar.

"Water's not going to cut it," I announce.

We arrive at the bar, and a bartender in his twenties with honey brown hair and warm brown eyes greets me. His jaw is scruffy, but in a neat way that says it's on purpose. "Hey there," he says in a soothing tone. "Anything you want. On the house."

Did he hear the sad story I told Hailey? I probably should've said that quieter. Now random strangers feel sorry for me.

"Oh, I couldn't do that. I'll pay." I reach for my purse, but I don't have it. I was minutes away from descending the grand staircase to start my life with my love, my best friend, and business partner. Yes, Dave is all three. *Was.* Shit. The business.

Just get through today. Business can wait until Monday.

"Open bar for the party," he says. "What can I get you?"

I haul my wedding gown up with me to a barstool. Luckily, there's no train, just layers and layers of tulle. I look like a frigging princess about to get my happy ending, only my prince turned out to be an ass. "Tequila."

"You got it," he says.

"Please," I add belatedly.

"And water too." Hailey perches on the stool next to me. "What can I do?"

I swallow over the lump of emotion in my throat. "Can you go back and tell everyone the wedding's off? I'm too embarrassed to explain."

"You have nothing to be embarrassed about," Hailey says firmly. "I'll take care of everything. You take all the time you need here, okay? You're in good hands with Cooper."

"Thanks," I manage.

She holds her palm out. "Here. I'll take your veil back and put it with your stuff."

"I don't want it."

"Okay. I'll take care of it for you."

I take a shaky breath. "Am I the first jilted bride you've had?"

"Sweetie, I've seen everything. Not all weddings go as planned, but usually that's for the best." She squeezes my shoulder, gives me another sympathetic look, and leaves.

Cooper slides the shot glass over to me, and I toss it back. I shudder, not used to hard alcohol. Cooper leans casually against the bar, studying me. Suddenly self-conscious, I wipe the tears from my face.

"Thanks for the drink," I say. "I'm Rowan."

"Nice to meet you, Rowan. I'm Cooper."

"Yeah, I heard. I mean, nice to meet you." I lift my glass. "Can I get another?"

He takes the glass. "Have you eaten today?"

"Only a wedge of cantaloupe this morning. I was too nervous."

"How does a burger and fries sound?"

I nearly drool. I've spent the past six months on a diet to make sure I fit into my wedding gown, which has a formfitting sleeveless bodice. I suppose I could've had the seams taken out, but I fell in love with it on the spot and didn't want to change a thing.

"That sounds great," I say. "I don't have any money on me, but I swear I'm good for it. I left my purse across the street at Ludbury House."

"No worries. I'll go put in the order."

He ambles to the kitchen in back. What a nice guy. And here I was thinking all men are scum. Welp, he's the exception that proves the rule.

Devastation hits me like a hammer, and I drop my head in my hands. *Dave, what happened?* We were in love. Hot tears sting my eyes. I thought I'd met the perfect man. Dave was charming, supportive, handsome. We were partners in life and in our shared advertising business in New York City. He was the face of our company, great with bringing in clients. It won't work without him.

Thinking back, things started to change about a month ago after Dave nearly drowned on a kayaking trip with friends. He started doing strange stuff. Like seeing a psychic, training for a marathon, and getting his balls waxed. Was he planning to join a strip show on his psychic's recommendation after running a marathon? Bizarre.

I tried to talk to him about it, but he said he was just living life to the fullest, and then made it seem like I was trying to hold him back and just needed to loosen up. Truth is, I couldn't let go of my dream of finally having a stable family of my own. We'd talked about having kids in the future. I so badly wanted things to be fine, I convinced myself they were.

I came out here to the suburbs of Clover Park, Connecticut, because I read great things about wedding planner Hailey Campbell and Ludbury House. Hailey's handled all kinds of weddings, even some high-profile clients. And she's great at making it a smooth, stress-free experience for the couple. How could I resist?

I prop my head in one hand, leaning against the bar. The tequila took the edge off. Is Dave seeing another woman?

He did seem distant at the rehearsal dinner last night. I thought he was just tired like I was. I take a sip of water and wish for tequila. What is taking that bartender so long? I glance around. I'm the only one at the bar now. Music blares from a back room. Seems like the party moved there. Some retro songs. It makes me think of my wedding reception that never was. It would've been full of music and dancing. Hailey and I planned every song, every moment together. I dash at another tear.

A short while later, Cooper appears from the kitchen carrying a tray with my burger and fries. He sets it in front of me. "I made this myself so you wouldn't have to wait as long."

"Really? Thanks." I take a bite of burger. *Mmmm, so good.* I keep eating, feeling less weepy by the moment.

After I finish the burger, I start on the fries. "You're a great cook."

"Thanks. Been working here a while."

I take a bite of fry. "I'm not usually so weepy. Normally, I'm in control, full steam ahead. You caught me on a really bad day."

He leans casually against the bar. "Sure. It's been a day."

A couple of twenty-something women approach the bar. Their facial features are similar enough to be sisters.

The brunette with blue eyes smiles at Cooper. "Could we get a couple of mojitos?"

His smile lights up his face. "You got it."

She turns to me. "Sorry about the day you're having."

I'm momentarily speechless. People are so friendly in this town. Also, word gets around fast. "Thanks."

The other woman with long honey-brown hair and hazel eyes says, "I hate your groom purely based on today's event."

"Thanks. I appreciate that." Look at how supportive these random strangers are to me! And where are my friends? I bolted without telling anyone what happened, but Hailey must've explained the situation by now and where I am. Darla, Meg, and I used to be close in high school, but then

Darla got married and moved to Kentucky. Meg's in the city with me. I guess I've been so busy building the business I didn't stay in touch with Meg as much as I should have. Still. I'm in crisis mode here. I go to text them and remember once again I left all my stuff at Ludbury House.

Guess I ultimately have to return to the scene of the crime. But not yet.

I watch as Cooper mixes the ladies' drinks and serves up a couple of beers to other people. I sip my water, a strange sense of lethargy taking over. I'm usually a high-energy, type A kind of person. All the buildup to the wedding only to have it blow up can really take it out of a person.

After the friendly women get their drinks, one of them says, "Take care."

And the other says, "Be strong," which makes me tear up.

"I will, thanks."

Now it's just me and Cooper again.

"Can I get you anything else?" he asks.

"I'm good with my water. Is it okay if I hang here for a while? I'm not ready to go back to Ludbury House to get my stuff."

"You hang here as long as you want. I'm glad for the company."

"Yeah?"

"Yeah, parties tend to be slow at the bar once everyone's had a couple of rounds."

"What's the party for?"

"Engagement party."

I put my hands up like blinders. "Not looking."

He chuckles. "Probably not the time for it. You want to talk about what happened? I'm a good listener."

"That's pretty much a prerequisite for a bartender, huh?"

"Here I thought I got the job for my mad cocktail skills."

I find myself smiling, which is a shock. I didn't think I could smile under the circumstances. And then all the horrible stuff comes crashing back, and I'm suddenly near tears again.

"Yeah, it's rough," he says, like he can read my freaking mind. "Totally get that."

I trace a line along the bar top before meeting his warm brown eyes. His expression is so understanding, it makes me want to confide in him. "I can't go home tonight. Dave will be there. We live together at his apartment."

"You can crash with me. I'll take the sofa, and you can have my room. I live in town."

I still. Clearly he didn't watch the same horror movie I did about a handsome stranger who invites a vulnerable woman to his place. Nope, not today, Satan.

Not that Cooper's Satan. I think he means well.

I answer politely but firmly. "That's very nice of you to offer, but I'll just ask a friend. Hopefully, they haven't left yet. I thought they'd show up here after Hailey told everyone."

He pulls his phone from his back pocket. "You want to text them?"

I reach for the phone, but then realize I don't have their numbers memorized. "Their numbers are programmed into my phone. I just need to get it." I gesture vaguely behind me. "Over there."

"I could get your stuff. Just let me know what I'm looking for."

"No, it's scattered around a messy bridal suite. I can do it."

I take a long drink of water, my limbs heavy. The energy it would take to get off this barstool, walk across the street, and face a fully decorated wedding is too much. "Maybe later."

"Sure."

"Tell me all about you. I'd like to stop spiraling about my doomsday."

His lips curve up. "Not much to tell. Grew up here in Clover Park, love it, never want to leave. Love working here."

"What else?"

"Let's see. I love basketball, playing it not watching it. Baseball's fun too. I take life as it comes, and life is good."

"You sound really happy."

"I am."

"More," I say.

He smiles gamely and goes on about his huge extended family and all the fun he had growing up with his cousins. I can't keep the names straight, there's too many of them. I just soak in the warmth of his voice with its deep soothing tone, drawing me into a different world full of love and good times.

Finally, he says, "And that's about it."

I stare at him for a long moment.

"What?"

"Do you know how rare that is? To love everything about your life? To have such a big happy family?"

"Well, we're not always happy. I gave you the highlight reel. There's been some rough stuff, but we stick together."

A sharp pang of envy hits me. He *belongs*. "So you've never left Clover Park?"

"Left for college. Came back. It's home."

"Wow. Deep roots."

"Guess you could say that."

I think back to the upheaval of my own childhood and quickly shut down that line of thought. I need to focus on the crisis I'm dealing with now.

A redheaded woman approaches the bar and says in a husky voice to Cooper, "There you are."

Cooper smiles, his voice warm. "Hey, Gina. How's it going?"

"Good. Is there some kind of event going on?"

"Yeah, but you can stick around if you want. What can I get you? Open bar, so it's on the house."

"Really? I'd love a pinot grigio."

"You got it." He goes for a wineglass and serves up her wine. "How're you liking the apartment?"

"Fantastic. I can't thank you enough."

"No thanks necessary. I know people for everything."

Her voice turns flirty. "You should stop by. See what I did with the place."

"I bet it's amazing."

"How about tonight?"

"Can't. Working late. Raincheck?"

"Sure." She takes a sip of wine and turns toward the dining area. "Oh my God, is that Shayla Adler? I love her movies."

"Yup, it's her engagement party."

She bolts.

Shayla Adler is here? I look over to see her wearing a small bridal veil pinned to her hair. Normally I'd want to meet her too, but not when she's in bride mode. I don't think I can force out a congratulations after getting dumped on my wedding day.

Solemn vow to self: no more men, ever.

Cooper checks in with me. "How're you doing? Want another water?"

I look down at my empty glass. "Probably time I left."

"Hold on." And then he surprises me by pushing through a half door at the side of the bar and joining me. "I'll go with you to get your stuff. I'm sure you'll feel better once you're in your regular clothes."

"But don't you have to work?"

"I'm a guest at this party. Everyone can help themselves."

My jaw drops. "A guest turned bartender? But you went into the kitchen too."

He laughs. "I work here, but I had tonight off for the party."

I gesture vaguely to where flirty Gina went. "But you told Gina you had to work late."

"Because I wanted to be here for you."

He offers his hand to help me off the barstool. I take it, a shock of sensation running up my arm at contact. *What was that?*

I quickly release his hand and check my gown to be sure it's not sticking up anywhere and exposing me.

He glances around me. "All covered. Let's go."

And then he offers his arm, like something out of a movie.

Who is this guy? He waits patiently while I stare at his arm and then at him.

His eyes are intent on mine. "The nice thing about holding my arm is that you don't have to worry about your heels getting caught in a sidewalk crack or in the brick path leading up to Ludbury House."

I gingerly place my hand on his arm, meeting hard muscle. Heat flashes through me. I must be out of sorts today. I've never reacted so viscerally to a simple touch. "How do you know about women stuff like heels?"

"My mom lives in heels." He guides me toward the door. "And I have a sister who complains about heels. She's the one who said she was sorry about the day you were having."

"Oh, I thought…never mind."

"What?"

"Several pretty women came to the bar and seemed happy to see you."

He holds the door open for me, guides me down the two steps, and places my hand back on his arm. "Guess I'm a likeable guy. My secret is I like everybody. People sense that, and then they want to like you too."

A silver Toyota slows down near us. The window powers down. It's my friend Meg, driving with Darla in the passenger seat.

Meg waves wildly. "Sorry! We waited as long as we could for you to come back, but we just heard Sam's in the hospital. His appendix burst. Darla wants to fly home right away, and I'm taking her to the airport." Sam's Darla's husband.

"Sorry!" Darla yells. "We'll talk soon, okay?"

"Yes, sure. Go ahead. I understand."

They take off. Didn't Hailey tell them I was at Happy Endings? Maybe they thought I'd go back to Ludbury House to get my stuff. What a wretched day. My eyes get hot, tears threatening.

"You okay?" Cooper asks.

I burst into tears once again. Dammit. This is not me.

Cooper puts a hand on my arm. "Is it okay if…"

I don't hear the rest of what he says over my sobs. My knees go weak. I just want to sink to the sidewalk and cry in a puddle of tulle.

"Ah!" My eyes open wide. Cooper just picked me up!

He carries me cradled in his arms. "I'm just expediting this operation. You go ahead and cry."

I lean into his warm chest and let the tears flow freely until I have nothing left. When I open my eyes, we're on the beautiful wraparound porch of Ludbury House. The white mansion is two and a half stories with columns in front.

He sets me down and opens the heavy wooden front door. "Unlocked." He holds it for me. I step inside, bracing myself to see all the silk streamers and flowers from my wedding.

"It's all cleaned up," I say in wonder.

"It's been a couple of hours."

"It has?"

He winks. "Time flies when you're hanging with a charming bartender."

"Thank you, Cooper. I'm going to go up and change."

"No problem. I'll wait here for you."

"You don't have to do that."

"Just want to make sure you land on your feet. Now's not the time to go it alone."

My throat tightens. "Thank you."

"No thanks needed."

I'm suddenly overwhelmed by the kindness and generosity he's shown me. I want to hug him but hold back because we just met. Of course, I just sobbed into his shirt for the time it took to get here while he held me in his arms. "I'll return the favor somehow."

He shakes his head. "It's not a transaction, Rowan. I don't expect anything in return. In fact, I don't want anything in return. I just want to know that you land in a safe place tonight."

My lips part as I remember he offered his place. And then

I remember how much I enjoyed touching him. My cheeks flush. *No more men, ever.*

I whirl, hurrying up the grand staircase.

2

Cooper

I check the time on my phone. Rowan's been up there for a half hour now. Mom and Mackenzie can take forever getting ready, so I get taking a while, but I figured Rowan would want to be out of here ASAP.

I debate going upstairs to check on her. I'll give her a few more minutes. Her former fiancé must be an idiot. Just spending the short amount of time I did with her today, I saw a smart, beautiful woman with grit. I know, I know, I shouldn't notice she's beautiful. Wrong time. But hey, I'm only human.

That doesn't mean I'm going to get involved with her. I can help, just not get too close. My last serious girlfriend was a mess when we met. I helped her get her life back together, and as soon as I did, she moved on.

I head to the kitchen in the back and look in the refrigerator. Mom usually stocks it with wedding leftovers for staff. Mmm, that chocolate cake looks good, all sliced and plated too. Maybe Rowan will want some.

I walk back to the foyer and admire the grand staircase. I spent a good part of my childhood running around this mansion. Whenever we had a day off from school, Mom would bring us kids here, where she keeps an office. My dream was to slide down the railing of the grand staircase. Unfortunately, Mom had eyes in the back of her head and thwarted every effort.

When I was nine, I slid down the stairs on an antique tray I found in one of the upstairs rooms. It was awesome. I nearly gave my five-year-old brother, Finn, the same awesome experience when Mom ruined all the fun. After that, we had to stay in her office while she worked. My older sister, Mackenzie, loved playing wedding planner in Mom's office. Now Mackenzie's anti-love. Irony.

I check the time again. Something's wrong. I jog upstairs and find my way to the bridal suite. The sound of Rowan's crying reaches me before I'm close enough to knock. This is exactly why I stuck around. She's in a bad place.

I knock. "Rowan, you doing okay in there?"

"Y-yes."

"Are you changed?"

"I guess so."

I open the door and step inside. She's sitting on the floor in jeans and a half-buttoned blouse that shows delectable cleavage. No socks or shoes. Nothing packed. She's just staring at her phone, crying.

I crouch next to her. "Hey, why don't I look for your socks and shoes while you button the rest of your shirt?"

She holds up her phone to me. "Meg and Darla texted and called, but nobody else."

"Who were you hoping to hear from?"

"I thought my dad and brother would care at least a little bit."

"Maybe they didn't know what to say."

She scowls and dashes at her tears. "Why are you so optimistic? I think they didn't give a crap about my happiness."

"Does it make you feel better to think that?"

"No!"

"Okay, then let's go with my explanation. Come on, let's get you off the floor." I help her up. She's tall for a woman, so when she stands at her full height, her face is close to mine. Desire stirs, and I ignore it, shifting away. I meet a lot of women, but it's been a while since I've felt like this. Hooked, wanting more, despite the circumstances. *Don't go there. Be smart.*

Her wedding gown is draped across an upholstered chair. Mom will donate it later.

I open the closet to find a blue dress, sneakers with socks tucked inside them, and a red suitcase with wheels. "Score." I set the suitcase aside and give her the socks and shoes.

"Dave took the rental car back to the city," she says. "I got a text from him."

The asshole left her stranded. What in the world did she see in this guy?

"I'll get you wherever you need to go," I say.

"I can take the train at some point." She plants her hands on her hips and looks around. "There's more stuff that's supposed to go in the suitcase. A makeup bag, hairstyling stuff, a mirror, perfume, my lucky rabbit."

I cock my head. "I thought it was a lucky rabbit's foot."

"That's barbaric. No. It's my lucky rabbit from when I was a kid. His name is Lucky, though I'm seriously reconsidering that for obvious reasons."

I don't see a rabbit anywhere. I look up. Lucky the rabbit is on top of the ceiling fan. I jump and grab him.

Rowan sighs. "Darla's been hiding that thing since high school. She thinks it's funny."

I hold the rabbit to my chest. "Nothing funny about dragging a stuffed rabbit around." I hold the rabbit up to my ear and turn to her. "Do you have some plush carrots? He says he's hungry."

She snatches it from me. "It's not like I display him. I just keep him in my suitcase. Never mind." She sets her suitcase on a long ottoman and tucks Lucky into a corner, gets her blue dress from the closet, and sets that inside too.

The vanity has a collection of makeup, so I go over, looking for the makeup bag. I find it on the floor behind the vanity. "What were your friends doing in here? Playing keep-away with your stuff?"

She shakes her head. "I threw it when Michaela, that's my fiancé's ex-girlfriend, came in to announce that Dave left because he decided he couldn't marry me after all."

"Did you throw anything else?"

"No. I'm not usually prone to fits of temper. If you had seen the smug look on her face, you'd have thrown something too."

"I'm sure. I'll go look for the rest of your stuff."

I go down the hall and check out the bathroom. There's all the hair stuff. They probably needed an outlet close to the mirror. I gather up gel, mousse, hairspray, and a curling iron and head back to her room.

She hangs her wedding gown in the closet.

"Found the hair stuff," I say. "Is that everything?"

She turns and dashes a tear from her cheek. "Yes. I'm just going to leave this here."

"Okay." *Mom will know what to do with it.*

I pack all the hair stuff in her suitcase and zip it closed. "How about some cake? I saw some in the refrigerator downstairs."

"My cake? The triple-layer chocolate with cherry filling?"

"I think so. Is that bad?"

"I was really looking forward to that cake."

"Okay, then. Let's go. I got the suitcase. Grab your purse."

She hesitates.

"Unless you'd rather go home. I can box some cake for you to go."

"Home is Dave's apartment. We just put a deposit down on a condo and got approved for a mortgage, but I can't swing it on one salary." She pinches the bridge of her nose. "I'm not sure where I'm going with this. I'm exhausted and not thinking straight."

"I can find you a place to stay tonight. Doesn't have to be with me."

She takes a deep breath. "I'd like to put off reality a little longer. Let's eat cake."

She grabs her large purse from the floor and heads out. I follow. She stops on the way to poke her head in the bathroom and gasps.

"Cooper! Why didn't you tell me I look like a raccoon? Look at my mascara and eyeliner. What a mess."

"It didn't seem important in the grand scheme of things." Honestly, it doesn't take away from her beauty.

She digs in her purse and finds a travel makeup wipe, expertly cleaning up her eyes. Then she flips it over and cleans her entire face.

She turns to me, fresh-faced and stunningly beautiful. "Better?"

"Yeah. Good. Great, actually." Her skin is flawless, her eyes a sparkling blue, her nose cute and upturned, her lips full and luscious. I can't seem to look away.

She gives me an uncertain smile. "Thanks."

She heads for the stairs. Halfway down, she says, "This was supposed to be my big moment on the grand staircase."

"Now it's a little moment on the way to better moments."

"Can I bottle your positivity?"

I lower my voice to a husky tone like they do in perfume ads. "Positivity by Cooper."

"People would spray that perfume everywhere. We'll make millions."

"Got that right."

We reach the foyer, and she gives me a small smile. She's a trooper. I take the lead toward the kitchen in the back of the mansion. There's a small table and chairs there for staff.

"Have a seat," I say, setting her suitcase nearby. I take the biggest cake slice from the refrigerator for us to share. Cool. There's champagne too. I bring both to the table. I'm sure it's from Rowan's wedding, so Mom wouldn't mind us taking it.

I go to the cabinet in search of glasses.

As I set her glass on the table, I see she's already swiped cherry filling from the cake with her finger. "Good?"

She nods, focused on picking the good stuff out.

I get out napkins and forks and set them on the table for us. Then I hold the champagne bottle up in question.

"Might as well. I sprang for the good stuff."

I pop the cork and pour a couple of glasses. After I join her at the table, I go in for a forkful of cake. She blocks me with both hands.

"I need my own slice," she says.

"Got it." Her slice is more like a huge slab, but now is not the time to mention that. I go for another smaller slice from the refrigerator.

I join her at the table and take a forkful. "Mmm, this is fantastic."

"I know," she says, not pausing in her careful dissection of the cake. Now she's using the fork to scoop all the filling from every layer, leaving the cake part in crumbles behind.

We eat in companionable silence. After her slab is nothing but hunks of cake—she exclusively ate the filling and icing—she sets her fork down.

"You don't like the cake part?" I ask.

"Not my favorite. I feel a little better now. Sugar rush is helping."

"Good."

She sips her champagne. "I went all out for this wedding in a stupid attempt to impress my father. We haven't spoken in years. I guess we still don't have much to say to each other. He left without a goodbye."

"Sorry to hear it."

She watches the bubbles in her champagne. "He's a workaholic corporate lawyer. Probably rushed home to get started on another case. Weekends are just another day for him. My brother has an equally impressive career. Cade's a neurosurgeon, and his wife's a psychiatrist."

"Are you close with your brother?"

She drinks more champagne. "Not really. We don't have much in common, and he's really busy. So am I. But hey, it's fine. Less chances for me to disappoint them." She sighs. "I'll never measure up to my family's expectations. I always fall short."

"Hey, don't be so hard on yourself. I'm sure you have many great qualities. I can tell already you're courageous. Some brides would've crumpled in a cloud of tulle."

She stares at me. "You know what tulle is?"

"Mom's a wedding planner."

Her eyes widen. "Hailey's your mom?"

"Didn't I mention that?"

"No. You don't look like her. I thought you were just the bartender."

I frown. "Just the bartender? I'll have you know I run the place with my dad. One day it'll be mine."

She holds up her palms. "No offense. It's a great place. I was just thrown by the fact that you're Hailey's son."

"I took after Dad more in looks."

"He must be handsome." She slaps a hand over her mouth like she can't believe she said that.

My lips curve up. "Thanks. Anyway, the reason I think you're courageous and strong is because instead of falling apart, you got mad and made it through an engagement party."

"That's because you distracted me from the festivities." She helps herself to chocolate icing from my cake. "I have to wonder, if I were raised differently, would I be massively successful by now like my brother?"

"By whose definition of success?"

"You know what I mean. He's a neurosurgeon. I run a small ad agency. It's profitable, but not where I want us to be."

"Wait. Weren't you raised the same way?"

She shakes her head. "I was raised by my grandmother. Cade was raised by Dad. Long story."

"Can I get the short version?"

"Mom died when I was twelve. Dad shipped me off to Grandmom and kept my brother."

My jaw drops. "Why?"

She meets my eyes and says matter-of-factly, "Because he didn't know how to raise a teenaged girl."

Whoa. She lost her mom, and then her dad abandoned her? I don't know what to say. I definitely don't want to make her feel worse after the day she's had.

"Did you like living with your grandmother?" It's the only neutral territory I can think of.

She swipes cherry filling from my cake and eats it. "Grandmom was overwhelmed with grief from the loss of her daughter and wanted me to take her place. How do you compete with a ghost?" She shrugs. "Mom was vice president of an ad agency. I run an ad agency. Best I could do."

"That's great. You should be proud."

"I run it with my ex."

I suppress a wince. "Just him?"

"Yup."

"That sucks."

"Mmm-hmmm." She stares at what's left of my cake and pushes back from the table. "I should go."

"Sure." I make short work of cleaning up the table and putting the dishes in the dishwasher.

"Wow. You're efficient."

"It's just like restaurant work. Dad started me off as a busboy, and I had to work my way up."

"What did you go to college for? I mean, your major."

"Business. I thought about working for a company, but every summer I worked at Happy Endings, and it just felt like that's where I belonged."

"I don't think I've ever known where I belonged." Her voice sounds small.

My instinct is to pull her close, but I already touched her enough, carrying her over here while she cried. Not gonna lie, I loved the feel of her in my arms, even though I felt terrible about her tears. *Boundaries.*

"You'll find where you belong," I assure her.

She's quiet on the walk back to Happy Endings, and I give her some space. I'm sure it's not easy to deal with a breakup and a work disaster at the same time. Not to mention she lives with the guy. Her whole life just imploded.

"My car's parked around back," I say when we get to Happy Endings. "I can take you to my parents' place for the night. They have a spare room."

She worries her bottom lip. "Nothing against your mom, but she was my wedding planner, and it's too soon for the reminder of all things wedding."

Just then Mackenzie and Harper come out of Happy Endings. My sister and cousin can help. I introduce them to Rowan.

Mackenzie glances at me and turns to Rowan. "Cooper's famous for rescuing women. How's he doing?"

Rowan's lips part in surprise. "Uh…good."

"I do not rescue women," I say defensively. "I just help out sometimes."

"They're usually beautiful too," Harper says.

Now I sound like an asshole who preys on beautiful women. "Well, Harp, it seems the beautiful ones often get the short end of the stick. Like Rowan here."

Rowan's hand goes to the side of her neck, her cheeks turning pink.

"Anyone could see you're beautiful," I tell her like it's an objective fact instead of an attraction growing by the minute. I turn to Mackenzie and Harper. "She needs a place to stay tonight. Would it be okay if she went to your place?"

"Oh, no, I couldn't," Rowan says. "I'll get a hotel."

"She lives with her ex-fiancé," I explain.

"Say no more," Harper says. "You're in."

"For sure," Mackenzie says. "We have a four-bedroom house, and it's just the two of us. Two of our roommates moved out."

Rowan looks from Mackenzie to Harper. "Are you sure? I mean, we just met."

"You met them earlier at the bar too," I say. "Sounds like a solid friendship."

"Sisters before misters is my philosophy," Mackenzie says. "You're a sister in need."

"And you don't look like an ax murderer," Harper says.

Rowan laughs a little. "I'm not."

"Are you allergic to cats?" Mackenzie asks.

Rowan shakes her head. "Dave is. I don't know why I just mentioned my ex. Who cares!"

"Then it's settled," Mackenzie says. "We live just around the corner. We can walk there."

I follow along. "Their cat is named Felix, and he only likes Mackenzie."

Rowan stops me with a hand on my arm, goes on tiptoe, and kisses my cheek. Warmth rushes through me. "Thank you, Cooper. I've got it from here." She takes her suitcase from me.

"Sure. You're in good hands."

I watch her go, a strange sense of longing coming over me. I did my part. Time to let go.

She turns and looks over her shoulder at me. Our gazes lock. There's something there between us. A pull. No, I'm done with wrecked women who use me and leave. Learned my lesson with Brianna.

She waves, and I wave back.

She turns the corner out of sight. I stand there for a moment in a daze before I snap out of it and walk back to Happy Endings, my home away from home.

As I walk to my car, it hits me that I didn't get her number. I don't even know her last name.

I may never see her again. My gut tightens. It's for the best. The timing isn't right. Timing is everything.

I get in my car and peel out of the lot.

∼

Rowan

I'm blown away by the kindness and generosity of everyone I've met in Clover Park so far. I follow the women down a tree-lined street with lovely Victorian homes. The sun's setting, giving everything a soft glow. This town is magical like something you'd see on a postcard.

Mackenzie and Harper talk animatedly about the engagement party and Shayla's upcoming wedding. The women look similar and are close in size, but Mackenzie has blue eyes and a sunny disposition while Harper has hazel eyes and a brash, take-no-shit attitude. Maybe I just get that impression because Harper went off on how long it took her brother Owen to get with the Shayla program. Her exact words: "finally got his head out of his ass."

"I'm sorry," Harper says to me. "Here we've been going on about Shayla and Owen's wedding after your awful day."

"No, it's okay. I get that you're excited. I'm sure it'll be very glamourous."

"Actually, it's at Ludbury House like your—sorry," Mackenzie finishes sheepishly. "No more wedding talk. I promise. Anyway, we're here."

We stop at a beautifully restored two-story home—white with dark green shutters and a wraparound porch. A porch swing draws my eye. I can just imagine working on the porch, feeling the breeze as I swing. Not that I'm staying here. Just one night, and then I have to face my ex and my living situation. Ugh. It's not going to be easy to untangle our lives since we live and work together.

"Welcome to Casa Campbell," Mackenzie says grandly as she opens the front door. She flips on light switches by the door.

I follow her in. "Thank you." The inside is just as lovely. We're in a front parlor room with a large fireplace, a red velvet sofa, and a TV on a short stand. The hardwood floors look original to the house. Through an archway, there's a living room done in a light yellow with crown molding. A brown leather sofa, upholstered chairs, and a reading nook in a bay window make the space inviting.

"I feel weird calling it Casa Campbell when Shayla bought the place," Harper says.

"Yes, but she signed the deed over to us," Mackenzie says.

"Shayla Adler bought you a house?" I ask.

"She bought it for herself and invited us to be her roommates," Harper says. "Then she moved in with Owen after they got engaged and signed it over."

"She used to live here with her assistant, Olivia," Mackenzie says. "Now it's just me and Harper rattling around the place, so we're glad to have your company."

I smile. "I'm happy you took me in. How do you know Shayla?"

"She lived with my family for the summer," Harper says. "My mom is Claire Jordan. Have you heard of her? Actor, producer, director. She knew Shayla from work and invited her to stay when Shayla was sixteen and getting in trouble out in LA."

"Your mom is Claire Jordan?!" She's a huge star in movies I've seen many times. They replay on TV. Now you don't see her as much.

"I know I don't look like her," Harper says. "I got her nose and chin, but the rest is Dad. Those Campbell genes run strong."

"Our dads are identical twins," Mackenzie says. "That's why we look similar, even though we're cousins."

"How about you?" Harper asks. "Your family nearby?"

"Dad's in the city. My brother's in Atlanta. Mom passed when I was a kid."

"So sorry," Mackenzie says.

"Sorry," Harper says. "I'll shut up now with the personal questions."

"You need a good night's rest," Mackenzie says to me. "I'm sure everything will seem more manageable in the morning."

"Wine?" Harper offers.

"Wine sounds great," I say.

I leave my suitcase in the parlor and follow the women into a modern kitchen done in white with silver accents.

"Take a seat," Mackenzie says, gesturing to a small round table.

I sit with my back in the corner like I always do. Just feels cozier that way. Safer. Mackenzie rounds up glasses, and Harper uncorks a bottle of wine.

They join me at the table. Harper pours. "It's sauvignon blanc."

"Sounds good," I say.

After we all have our drinks, Harper raises her glass. "Drink up, bitches!"

"To friends," Mackenzie says.

I clink their glasses, and we all take a sip. They look at me expectantly. I'm sure they're curious about me. "So what do you ladies do?"

"I'm a graphic designer," Harper says.

"I'm a partner in a high-tech security firm," Mackenzie says, "with my cousin Owen, Shayla's fiancé—"

"He's my brother," Harper says.

"And my other partner is a family friend, Nathan," Mackenzie says.

"Nathan Brooks is death to every party," Harper says. "I asked you to call him Nat so I can swat him away."

"Nat, gnat," Mackenzie says like that explains the mystery that is Nathan.

Mackenzie drinks some wine and says brightly, "I basically run the place, bring in new business, marketing, accounting, logistics. The guys install the security systems and secure tech. They used to be hackers. We have a good assistant, so that also helps."

"I work in the city, but they let me work from home most days," Harper says.

"How about you?" Mackenzie asks.

"I run an ad agency. It's small. Just me and—" My voice catches unexpectedly, and I take a drink.

"Your ex," Harper finishes for me.

I nod.

Harper shakes her head. "Damn, I don't envy you living and working with the guy who just screwed you over."

I press my lips together, a welcome anger returning. "He did screw me over."

"Then you avoided a disaster," Mackenzie says. "Better off without him."

"Single's where it's at," Harper says.

"I've dedicated my twenties to casual fun," Mackenzie says.

"She means casual sex," Harper says.

I laugh, surprising myself.

Harper gives me a conspiratorial look. "The worst part is, her mom's a wedding planner and a born matchmaker. Mac's rebelling." Hailey's daughter, of course.

"Mac is a truck," Mackenzie returns. "I'm not rebelling. I just don't believe in love."

"Yes, you do," Harper shoots back. "You got burned and shut everything down."

"You're one to talk."

They give each other side-eye and turn back to me. They remind me of siblings. Kinda funny. I never got to experience that special sister bond. I would've loved a sister.

"Did Cooper give you a tour of the town?" Mackenzie asks.

"We saw him carrying you down the sidewalk," Harper says.

A rare blush creeps up my neck. "Oh. I didn't know everyone saw that."

"We weren't spying," Mackenzie says. "We were at the bar helping ourselves and happened to see you because we were facing in that direction."

"Her dad owns the bar, so she can help herself whenever," Harper says.

"It was an open bar anyway," Mackenzie says.

They look at me expectantly.

I take a sip of wine. "No tour of the town. I, uh, got more bad news and sort of lost it on the sidewalk. He carried me across the street to Ludbury House to get my stuff."

Mackenzie shakes her head. "More bad news! What was it?"

"You don't have to answer," Harper says, shooting Mackenzie a look.

I hold up a palm. "No, it's fine. My friends left early because of an emergency. I just felt sort of stranded."

"Well, you landed in the right place," Mackenzie says.

I smile. "I'm getting that feeling. So does Cooper really rescue women all the time?"

"Frequently," Harper says.

"For a kid who ran wild—" Mackenzie starts.

"He used to throw food at us, even as a teenager," Harper says.

"He turned into a good guy," Mackenzie finishes.

Cooper's warmth and generosity meant everything to me. Not sure how I feel about being one of many wrecked women he fixes up. He made me feel sorta special. Silly. After the overwhelm of my day, I'm not thinking clearly.

The conversation moves to a mystery series they've been watching, which just happens to be one of my favorites too.

I warm to the topic. "Only problem is, I watch it late at night on my laptop and fall asleep before I find out whodunit. I'm usually so tired from putting in long hours at work."

"Work, shmerk," Harper says. "Do you want to get paid or find out whodunit?"

We laugh.

"I think I'm going to get ready for bed," I say. "It's been a hellish long day."

Mackenzie stands. "I'll make up a room for you."

"Thanks, both of you. I really appreciate it."

A short while later, I crash into a comfortable bed and sigh. My mind bounces from one dire thought to another. Reality crashing in on me. The expense of the wedding for nothing, the stunning breakup with no warning, needing to move my stuff out of Dave's apartment, finding a new place I can afford on my own, the business. My vision of the future is shattered.

My nerves are raw, anxiety forming a tight ball in my chest. Where do I go from here?

Mee-rrowr! Mee-rrowr! Mee-rrowr!

I jackknife up in bed. The high-pitched cry sounds like a cat in distress. Mackenzie did say she had a cat. Felix, that's right.

I open my door. A gray cat with a white mustache and white chest stares at me. There's a small pink toy monkey in front of him. He picks up the monkey and drops it on my foot.

"Did you hunt for me? Thank you. Goodnight."

I turn to go, and the cat zips past me into the room. "I thought you only liked Mackenzie." I scoop him up, and he goes limp. I carry him out to the hallway and kick his pink monkey across the hall. There. I shut the door and pad back to bed.

Ahhh. Now I can sleep.

Mee-rrowr! Mee-rrowr! Mee-rrowr!

I roll to my side and cover my ears with the pillow.

Mee-rrowr! Mee-rrowr! Mee-rrowr! He's getting louder and more insistent.

I roll out of bed, stride over, and open the door. The pink monkey is back. He drops it on my foot.

I pick it up. "Thank you, Felix. Goodnight." This time I slip inside, keeping my foot blocking the entrance so he can't get in. Eww, the monkey is ratty and damp. I drop it on the floor.

I'm not even back in bed before he starts again, only now it's caterwauling. It sounds like a baby crying.

I march to the door and fling it open. "What?"

Felix runs in, ignoring the monkey, and jumps on my bed. He curls up on my pillow.

I leave the door open so he can leave when he gets bored. Then I set him on the floor, get in bed, and stare at the ceiling. I'm so exhausted. I just want to—ah!

I yelp as Felix lands on my chest. He stretches across my torso, resting his head between his paws and staring at me. I reach out and rub the side of his cheek. He leans into my hand and purrs. I guess it's not so bad having a warm cat purring on me.

I pet him, glad for the sweet company. "I'll figure things out in the morning."

He yawns.

I crash into sleep and dream of chasing a groom through the zoo and landing in the lion's den. I wake in a cold sweat, breathing hard, confused about where I am.

I spot Felix curled up next to me on the bed. Right. Mackenzie and Harper's place. Clover Park. My disaster of a wedding.

I punch the pillow and flop down again. *Go to hell, Dave. And stay out of my dreams!*

3

As soon as I wake up, I cancel my business credit card and get a new one. The old one was in my name only because Dave had bad credit for defaulting on student loans. I got him an employee card on my account. I'll go to the bank on Monday to open a solo business bank account and transfer my half of the money from our joint business bank account. Not that there's a lot in there. Most of what we made, I invested back in the business. I don't want Dave having access to my half of the money. I no longer trust him.

That taken care of, I go to the kitchen in search of coffee and find Mackenzie getting the coffeemaker going. She's in running clothes, her long brown hair up in a high ponytail.

She smiles. "Hey, Rowan. How'd you sleep?"

"Not too bad. I'm just happy I slept at all."

"Every day will get a teensy bit easier."

"Are you as full of positivity as your brother?"

She gets two thick white mugs from the cabinet. "Probably. You met my mom. She's always looking to the bright side, full of hope. I think it's, like, a rule for a wedding planner."

Felix winds around my leg, and I stroke him behind the ear.

"I can't believe how friendly he is with you," Mackenzie

says. "It seemed like he picked me to be his person and couldn't be bothered with anyone else."

"He brought me his pink monkey last night."

"Oh, Felix! Sorry about that. Usually he brings it to my room every night. You went to bed earlier, so I guess he thought he'd try it on you." She reaches over and pets Felix, who leans into her hand.

The coffeemaker beeps. Mackenzie pours us both coffee and heads for the table. I join her.

"So what's your plan for today?" Mackenzie asks.

"I need to get back to my apartment in the city to get some of my stuff, my laptop most importantly. I guess that's as good a time as any to talk to Dave."

"You think he'll be home?"

"His Sunday routine is like clockwork. Sleep in, work out, shower, and go across the street to the Irish pub until dinner."

"Is he an alcoholic?"

"I don't think so. He likes the audience for his stories."

She takes a sip of coffee. "Harper and I can go with you and help bring your stuff back."

I consider the offer. "Thanks, but I think it's something I need to do myself."

"Sure, no problem. You're welcome to spend another night with us."

"Thanks. I really appreciate it."

Harper walks in, rubbing her eye and giving a big yawn. "Morning. What's up?"

"I'm spending another night," I say.

"Awesome. Coffee." She makes a beeline for the coffeemaker.

"Who wants pancakes?" Mackenzie asks brightly.

"Me," Harper says.

"Sounds great," I say.

Mackenzie goes for the ingredients while Harper joins me at the table. She jerks her thumb toward Mackenzie. "She's such a morning person. You're an alien species, Mac."

"Mac is a burger. I'm Mackenzie." She turns back to the counter, measuring ingredients. "I'll make eggs too."

A short while later, she slides a plate in front of me. Wow. There's a stack of three golden fluffy pancakes and perfectly cooked scrambled eggs with some kind of herb. "Thank you. What's this?" I point to the herb.

"Dill."

Harper plunks maple syrup in front of me and goes to the counter for her breakfast.

I pour the syrup on and take a bite. "Perfect."

Mackenzie smiles warmly and goes back to the stove.

I haven't felt taken care of in so long. It's always been me doing the caretaking. First for Grandmom and then for a long line of boyfriends who always ended up leaving me. Why am I drawn to people who need me to do all the work of caring for them? Never again. Dave is the final straw on top of everyone else who's abandoned me in my life.

Is there something unlovable about me that makes everyone leave?

I didn't realize I said that last bit out loud until I'm suddenly flanked by Mackenzie and Harper, squished into a group hug. I'm sitting, so I'm sorta pressed against their sides.

Mackenzie looks down at me. "There's nothing wrong with you."

"Don't let him get in your head," Harper says fiercely. "He's the asshole here. Not you."

"Why're you both so nice to me?" I ask, sincerely baffled by the solidarity and friendship.

"Because we're decent human beings," Harper says.

"We really feel for you," Mackenzie says. "If I were going through what you are, I'd want someone to be there for me in my time of need."

My throat tightens. "Thank you. One day I'll find a way to repay you both."

"You can clean the litterbox," Harper says.

Mackenzie shoves Harper's shoulder. "Rowan, you don't

have to do that. Geez, why not ask her to scrub toilets?" She returns to the stove.

"Isn't that what I just did?" Harper asks.

I go back to eating pancakes. Their easy banter makes me feel like I'm part of a family for the first time in a long time.

I'm in the city by early afternoon and walk briskly to the brownstone, where we have an apartment on the third floor. My gut churns.

Okay, I just need to get the most important stuff and go. I'll come back with a moving truck for the rest once I know where I'm going to live. We put a deposit on a condo, but we don't own it yet. We were going to close the deal after we got back from our honeymoon. I can't afford the mortgage payments without Dave. Hopefully, it won't take too long to get the deposit back. Add that to my to-do list for Monday.

I stop on the sidewalk, look up at our apartment, and take a deep breath. Here we go. I do the code on the keypad, go inside, and walk up to the third floor.

Once I'm inside our apartment, I look around. "Dave?"

Nothing. Good. I timed this well.

I head to the bedroom for my laptop. It's not on the nightstand shelf where I left it. My heart pounds. I have everything on that laptop. All client presentations and company records. When was the last time I backed it up? I can't remember. Okay, okay, don't panic. Maybe I didn't put it back in its usual spot.

I look around the small bedroom. There's not too many places it could be. I search through every dresser drawer and even look under furniture.

No, no, no. I yank the comforter off the bed and pat down the sheet, looking for a laptop-shaped lump. Panic drives me to the bathroom, searching in the vanity drawer.

I race to the living room, searching under cushions, in the

coffee table drawer, even behind the sofa. Sweat runs down my spine. He stole my laptop. It has to be.

Kitchen! I check all the cabinets and drawers, and move on to the refrigerator and freezer.

What else did he steal? My noise-cancelling headphones? I need those to focus. I rush back to the living room, where they're usually on the end table. Not there. I don't remember seeing them on my previous search. Mom's jewelry!

My breath comes faster as I make my way to the bathroom. I keep Mom's pearl necklace and diamond earrings in a velvet pouch in the vanity. It's the only thing I have of hers. My dad gave them to me after she died because he thought I might get some use out of them. I never wear them, but I've carried them from place to place with me.

I slowly pull open the vanity drawer, my heart thundering in my ears. Dave knows what this jewelry means to me. I pull out the velvet pouch and instantly know by its lightness it's empty. I turn it inside out to be sure. Gone.

I stand there, heart pounding, muscles tense for a long moment of shock. Dammit. I whirl and march out the door. Time to confront Dave.

I grab my purse and race out the door of the apartment, run down the stairs, and burst outside. A quick glance for traffic, and I run across the street to Riley's Pub, where Dave likes to entertain the bar crowd with his stories.

I barrel through the door and find him at the bar with a beer. A few guys near him laugh at something he said.

"Excuse me," I say, working my way past people to get to him.

His eyes widen when I invade his space. He plays it casual. "Hey, Rowan, this probably isn't the best time to meet up. I'll text you for a better time."

I clench my jaw. "I want my laptop, headphones, and jewelry back."

"I'm meeting someone."

"I don't care."

He gestures toward a quiet corner of the pub before grabbing his beer and moving to a table for two.

I march over and stand towering over him. It takes all of my willpower not to slap him. "Where is my stuff?"

"Take a seat, and I'll tell you."

I pull a chair out and sit.

Then he says with a straight face, "I hocked it."

I do a double take. "You hocked it? Where?"

"Buddy of mine has connections."

My jaw clenches. "I feel like I don't even know you. Why would you hock it? Why did you wait until the wedding to bail?"

He shakes his head. "I'm real sorry about the timing at the wedding. This isn't easy to say, but I was trying to decide who I was supposed to be with. I didn't know for sure until I was facing a lifetime with you. No offense."

"Oh, no offense taken," I snap. "Who is she? How long has this been going on?"

"About a month."

"You blew up our lives for someone you just met?"

He shrugs. "It's not like I planned it. It just happened."

"I'll be sending you the paperwork to dissolve our business partnership and a bill for the stuff you hocked without my permission."

"That money is gone."

"Already?"

"Yeah, I needed it to put a deposit down on Sheila's llama farm. It was a grand gesture to convince her of my sincerity."

"Who the hell is Sheila?"

"My esthetician."

My eyes widen. "The woman who waxes your balls?"

"She has many skills." He looks past me and waves. "She's here now. I told you this wasn't the best time."

I turn to see a stunning brunette in a flowing blouse and skinny jeans walking toward us.

"Am I interrupting?" she asks innocently. Like she doesn't know Dave dumped me on our wedding day.

"No, baby, stick around," Dave says. He turns to me. "You need to get your stuff out of my apartment by next weekend. Sheila's moving in."

"Who will take care of the llamas?" I ask sarcastically.

"My brother will live there," Sheila says. "For us, it'll be a country escape."

I stand so fast I knock my chair backward. "You messed with the wrong woman."

Dave puts out a placating hand. "Rowan, it was a tough decision between the two of you, if that helps."

Sheila turns to me. "No hard feelings, okay?"

I whirl and run from the pub, anger fueling me.

I head back to the apartment and grab my gym bag from the closet and stuff as many of my clothes into it as I can. I should've brought my suitcase from Mackenzie and Harper's place, but I was so focused on dealing with Dave, I wasn't thinking straight.

The sofa is mine, as is the coffee table, end table, and the flat-screen TV. Also, the stools at the breakfast bar and the living room area rug. Dave's stuff wasn't as nice as mine, so he got rid of it when I moved in. The bedroom furniture was his.

I dash at a tear and head for the kitchen for a plastic bag. Then I go to the bathroom and dump all of my toiletries and makeup into it. I briefly consider trashing his stuff, but I don't have the energy. Adrenaline leaks out of me, along with my fury. The wedding disaster, the new woman taking my place, hocking my treasures. It's suddenly all too much.

My eye catches on his hair-growth cream. Impulsively, I drop it in my bag. *I hope you go bald in a week!* It's a small thing, but the man is extremely sensitive about his thinning hair. He's thirty-two, so he's probably fighting genetics at this point.

I toss my bag over my shoulder and walk out the door, telling myself this is for the best. I don't want to be with a man who would flake on a marriage or his family. I can't believe I bought into the fantasy of a rosy future with him.

Serious denial on my part. I let him walk all over me, while he did whatever the hell he felt like. I was all give while he was all take. I'm seeing clearly now, and I'll never let myself be treated like that again.

I'd rather be alone than be with the wrong man. With any man, actually. Maybe I'll get a cat.

4

The next day is Monday, and I'm on fire taking care of business. *Bam! Bam! Bam!* I call Bob, the lawyer who drew up our business partnership papers, and have him get started on dissolving them. Next, I head back to the city to transfer my half of the business checking to a solo account, and I stop by the police station to report Dave for stealing my personal items. We weren't married, so that wasn't community property. It was mine, and he had no right.

Unfortunately, the officer explained it was complicated in a cohabitation situation, and I have no proof it was him. It's basically Dave's word against mine. She told me to try small claims court, which I definitely will. Of course, nothing can replace Mom's jewelry. Every time I think about it, my chest aches. Just one more reason Dave should burn in hell.

I grab a snack from a street vendor and head to a store for a new laptop, putting it on my credit card. One more bit of business as I walk to the train station—a call to the real estate company. I need the deposit money back on the condo to afford my own place. I get a guy named Matthew, who has zero sympathy for my newly single and homeless status as he informs me I'll get the deposit back in thirty days.

"Thirty days?" I exclaim. "I can't wait thirty days. You can easily sell the condo to another person. We never closed."

"It's in an escrow account. Thirty days is the best I can do. You're not the only one we do business with, Miss Sanders. We're a very busy firm."

"I'd like to talk to your supervisor."

"She's on vacation. You won't get a different answer. I have to put the request through accounting. There's a procedure in place here to keep things running smoothly. We could put that money toward another condo if you'd like to move quickly on a new place. This is a very hot market."

"No, I need the money back in my account."

"Very well, expect it in thirty days."

I grumble a thanks and hang up. Thirty days. It's not ideal, but it's something. Maybe I can stay in Clover Park a little longer. My friend Meg offered to let me stay in her apartment in the city, but she already has three roommates, which means I'd get the floor. Also, one bathroom for two guys and three women would be tough.

As soon as I have my condo deposit back, I can look for another apartment. I'll need to find a roommate to afford it or move someplace small and probably not in a good area. It's not ideal, but that's city life. One day, I'll be able to afford someplace nice by myself.

After growing up in a rural area of Pennsylvania with Grandmom and the suburbs of New Jersey before that, living in New York City was always the dream. The energy, the awesome food, always having something to do. I don't want to give that up. On the other hand, there's so many memories there of my life with Dave. No, I can't let Dave ruin everything for me. It's a big city, room enough for both of us.

Legally, Dave's entitled to half of the deposit from the condo. Considering he stole my stuff, some of which can never be replaced, I'm inclined to keep all of the deposit. But I won't stoop to his level. I don't steal or cut corners. Everything aboveboard, legal and clear. Rise above.

I take the train back to Clover Park and let out a breath as the city disappears from view. It'll get easier with time. I have to believe that. I still need to deal with the bill for our wedding. Why did I go all out for my wedding? I fell in love with Ludbury House, yes, but it was also a misguided attempt to show Dad I was doing well and get his approval.

That worked out about as well as my other attempts to make Dad proud. I don't know why I care anymore. Dad and Cade didn't care enough to see how I was doing after the wedding was called off. I'm the one who stays in touch with them. They're too busy to bother. Growing up, I saw them on holidays and two weeks in the summer. That's it. And I always felt like the third wheel.

When the train gets back to Clover Park, I ride Mackenzie's bike back to their house. It's a cute turquoise bike with a basket and a bell. There's a busy road to cross, but the rest of the ride is beautiful on winding tree-lined roads. The breeze plays with my hair, making me feel lighter and free. I can breathe here. It's probably just nostalgia for a quieter time of my life, but this countryside soothes my soul.

Now that it's October, the leaves are starting to change—bright reds, oranges, and yellows. If you have to have your life implode, this is a nice place to recover.

Once Main Street comes into view, I give myself a pat on the back for finding my way home. My temporary home, if Mackenzie and Harper agree to let me stay longer. Mackenzie did trust me with an extra house key.

No one's home when I get back. Probably both at work. The quiet is a little unnerving. I settle into the living room on a cushy brown leather sofa. I yelp as Felix leaps on my lap. He gives me a perturbed look before kneading my sweater.

I pet him under the chin. "Felix, you need a bell."

I need to get back to work too. We shut down the business for a week for the honeymoon, so as far as the clients know, everything is normal.

I slowly shift to get my new laptop. Felix jumps off my lap, annoyed. "Sorry, I'm taking care of business."

I boot up the laptop and log into my backup service, which apparently I haven't uploaded to in a month because, you guessed it, too busy with work and the wedding. I backup manually because one time the automatic backup screwed up the files and overwrote stuff I needed. Now I double-check everything before backing up. All is not lost. I can recreate anything I need, or maybe I'll find what I need in email.

Hope fills me for the first time in days. I have all my client contacts here. I'll just get in touch, tell them I'm a solo operation now as…the Sanders Agency. Butterflies dance in my stomach. Dave was the face of the company who brought in new business. He's great with charming people. I work best on strategy and implementation. I confess to a teensy bit of doubt about running the business solo. I'm not great at networking and closing the deal.

Okay, I'm not starting from scratch. We have clients already.

"This can work," I tell Felix as he gives his privates a bath on the floor nearby. He doesn't bother to look up.

I do a blind cc email to all of my clients and tell them the good news is, I'm back early from vacation. And also operating solo now. They don't need all the nitty-gritty details.

I wait for a response, hitting refresh obsessively. Okay, it's a Monday; they're busy. Understandable. I'll just go for a walk, and by the time I'm finished, surely someone will have gotten back to me. Right?

I get my purse from the front room and head out the door. I halt on the porch, suddenly realizing I don't have a destination. I could take a walk down Main Street, but I can only window-shop. I need to be frugal until I get that deposit back. I still owe a lot for the wedding too.

I settle on the porch swing. Oh, I know what to do while I wait. I have a book on my phone I can read. I tap over to my reading library and find my latest read, a book on taking your business to the next level. Look at me already working toward improving my business.

After an hour, I stand and stretch. Time to check email. Fingers crossed.

There's an email from Nikki. My breath catches as I read

her email: *Sorry, Dave offered a sweet deal to move over to Endeavor Media, so I'm with them now.*

The breath whooshes from my lungs. That's his cousin's company. Dave used to work there before he met me and we decided to start our own agency.

Clients are free to go at any time, of course, but isn't there a law against an employee taking the business with them somewhere else? Yes, I'm aware that's what I was hoping to do, but come on. After what Dave put me through, I should at least get to keep my job.

I shoot back an email to Nikki. *What was the sweet deal?*

No reply, but two more emails come in from other clients saying they're with Endeavor Media now. Adrenaline rushes through me. I race down the steps and to the sidewalk, running as hard as I can with no idea where I'm going. I just run in a straight line, passing houses, a dog park, more houses.

I hear footsteps pounding behind me and turn to see who else is running as hard as I am. Cooper. My rescuer from what I thought was a hellish day. Now being a jilted bride seems like a picnic compared to the devastation Dave has wrought.

"Hey, out for a run?" he says, not even winded. He's in a snug T-shirt that emphasizes the swell of his shoulders. His arms are corded with muscle. His legs too, which I have a good view of in his basketball shorts. I can't believe I even notice his good looks, but there you go. Lust works even when your life is falling apart. Guess that's what keeps the human race going.

He winks. "Silly question. You're running, so obviously you're out for a run. How're you doing?"

It's not just lust that draws me in. It's goodness. Cooper's a good guy. I think. Oh, what the hell do I know? I thought Dave was a great guy for the two years we were together. He was easy to live with, easy to work with, though it occurs to me I did the lion's share of work both at home and at the office, so of course he'd like that. And then he hopped in bed with his waxer lady. It sounds so ridiculous I'd laugh if I could. The sting in my eyes tells me it's a matter of seconds before I sob all over Cooper's shirt. Oh God, I don't want to cry in front of him again.

"Rowan?"

"Sorry, I've got a lot going on," I say in as calm a voice as I can muster. "Bit distracted."

He nods. "I was just on my way home. Want to come in for a drink?"

And because I'm feeling desperately alone at the moment, I hear myself say, "I'd love that."

"Should we run there? It's a few more blocks straight ahead."

"Sure." I start at a slow jog, and he keeps pace.

"Heard you were still in town. Did you get your stuff from your ex's apartment?"

I slow to a walk. He does too. "Not all of it. I have to rent a truck and get it this weekend. Dave says his new girlfriend's moving in."

"What an ass. Need some help?"

I do a double take. "You want to help me move?"

"Sure. I'll get my brother, Finn. He's in college in the city, so he can stop by."

I consider the alternative, hiring someone. It seems wise to save for an emergency like, say, food. Damn, I really am screwed. And here's Cooper appearing out of thin air just when I need him the most.

"That sounds great," I say. "Once again, thank you for your kindness and generosity."

His brown eyes twinkle with good humor. "So are we talking a baby grand piano or…"

I laugh. "Nothing that heavy."

Cooper

I can't take my eyes off her. We're sitting at the small table in my kitchen with glasses of water. I have the first-floor apartment of a house, the same apartment Dad used to rent. He's the one who told me about it when I came back to town for good. As luck would have it, the tenant was leaving at the end of the month.

Rowan's flushed from running, giving her a glow. She's so beautiful.

She puts a hand self-consciously to her cheek. "What? Is there something on my face?"

"Sorry, didn't mean to stare. Just lost in thought. I've been wondering how you're doing after, you know, the whole wedding thing."

"Ooh, it's gotten so much worse than just the wedding thing."

"What do you mean?"

And then she launches into a horrific story of Dave hocking her late mother's jewelry among other valuables and stealing their clients. Not to mention he was cheating on her.

A cold rage bubbles through me. And I'm not an angry person. I want to throttle this guy and then pull Rowan close and protect her from everyone and everything.

She holds her palms up. "Welcome to my life."

"I'm so sorry. I can't fathom what kind of person would do that."

"A self-centered man with zero integrity. He was great until suddenly he wasn't. Obviously I was in denial."

I shake my head. "He can't get away with this."

"He already did. I'm taking him to small claims court for hocking my stuff, but the rest of it, well, I'm not sure I can do anything more. I suppose I could try to woo my clients back, but if Endeavor Media's offering a cut-rate deal, I can't match that and stay in business."

"So you think you'll stick around Clover Park for a while?" I ask.

"I was thinking about it. I have to wait thirty days to get my condo deposit back, which I need to get another place."

"There's an apartment opening up on the second floor

here, if you're interested. One bedroom, shared backyard. Utilities included."

"How much?"

When I tell her, her jaw drops. I laugh. "It's not city prices."

"I'll say. That would get me a crappy apartment in a seedy area of the city, and I'd have to get two roommates."

"Want the landlord's info?"

Our gazes lock for a charged moment. She looks away, her hand fluttering in the air. "I'm not planning to stay that long. I was hoping Mackenzie and Harper wouldn't mind too much if I stayed with them for a month."

"So you must be getting along with them."

She meets my eyes. "They've been wonderful. Just like you."

"Must be something in the water," I say, lifting my glass of water and taking a drink.

She doesn't drink. That would've been a nice touch.

"I'm sure they wouldn't mind if you stayed with them for a while," I say. "Keeps them from bickering too much."

"I'll ask. Of course I'd pay rent and utilities."

"I doubt they'll charge you rent. The house is paid off. They're just covering utilities and food."

"And property taxes too, I'm sure. I'll give what I can and clean the litterbox."

I laugh. "You don't have to clean the litterbox."

"It's the least I can do. Besides, Felix is my new best bud."

"I thought I was your new best bud."

She flashes an impish smile. "I haven't heard you purr."

I do my best approximation of a purr. She strokes my hair like she's petting me and quickly drops her hand.

Her eyes meet mine and shift away. "Almost as soft as Felix."

I bite back the many pussycat references on the tip of my tongue.

She lets out a shaky breath. "Is it weird I feel sorta free

right now? Like I'm getting an unexpected fresh start. It's terrifying but also exhilarating."

"I'm liking the optimism creeping in. I knew you had grit."

She cocks her head. "I guess I do. If only I had better instincts for people."

"Your instincts are just fine." I lean across the table and lower my voice to a husky tone. "You're here with me, aren't you?"

She flushes. "It's too bad I didn't meet you before Dave. You seem like the kind of guy I should've been with. Now it's too late."

"Why is it too late?"

"Because I never want another relationship ever."

"Never ever?"

She swats my arm. "Don't tease. I'm serious. My heart is shattered into tiny sharp pieces that stab me every time I breathe."

"Then you're in luck. I'm not only a bartender and cook, I'm a handyman. I can fix it."

She shakes her head. "It's too far gone."

I lean forward. "Rowan, I can fix your heart." Her breath hitches. This is definitely not one sided.

She looks down, tracing a circle on the table.

I go for casual to put her at ease. "Proof of my handyman skills is in Mackenzie and Harper's house. When Shayla first bought the house, I was the one who went through and fixed anything that needed fixing, installed closet organizers, and helped assemble furniture."

She meets my eyes. "Living up to your handyman title. And that was so nice of you to do."

"They paid me with a thank you. My brother, Finn, got paid big bucks to paint the interior. What's that about?"

She cocks her head. "That's strange."

"Nah, it was actually a funny situation. They were origi-nally paying him so he could earn money for a car, but then he developed this ridiculous crush on Olivia, Shayla's assistant, who, by the way, is four years older than him. Finn's still in college. Anyway, Olivia found it disturbing that Finn was crushing on her, so she got Shayla to pay him triple overtime to finish the job faster."

"Aww, I bet he's as sweet as you."

"Yeah, you think I'm sweet? What else?"

She pushes back from the table. "I should go." She gestures vaguely behind her. "Stuff to do."

I stand. "You in the mood for ice cream? We could grab some on the way back to your place. Shane's Scoops is the premier ice-cream place in the state. They've won awards. It's right on Main Street. Everything's homemade, even the mix-ins."

She melts on the spot. "I would love ice cream. I've been having such a craving."

I lead the way out. "Not surprised."

"How many flavors do they have?"

"I never counted." I open the door for her and lock it behind us. "A lot."

"Do they have chocolate cherry?" she asks with such hope in her eyes I can't bear to disappoint her.

"I have no idea, but I will search the entire state to find you some."

She puts a hand on my arm. "No wonder women are falling all over you."

"What women?"

"Just about every woman who walks into your bar."

"That's not true."

"It's because you care."

I meet her eyes. "I care about you."

She looks away and hurries down the sidewalk. "Come on, ice cream awaits. I need to ruin my running workout as soon as possible."

They say the way to a man's heart is his stomach. Women are exactly the same with a twist. The way to a woman's heart is chocolate.

5

Rowan

After indulging in chocolate cherry ice cream from the best ice-cream shop in the state, I go home on a sugar high, determined to win my clients back.

First call is to Brian, a friendly guy who's always a pleasure to work with. He owns a catering business in the city.

"Hi, Brian, it's Rowan Sanders. I understand Endeavor Media made you a discounted offer to stick with them for a year. Sometimes you get what you pay for. I think you'll agree I achieved great results with your social media campaign and online marketing for your business."

"Yeah. We were happy with your work, but our budget's tight, and we can't turn down Endeavor's offer. Twenty-five percent off for a year is an incredible deal. They're an established firm. Maybe after our year discount is up, we could talk again."

"Of course, keep in touch."

"Sorry to hear about you and Dave."

Guess Dave let our clients know we were going our separate ways when he made the deal. He sure worked fast. Makes me wonder if he did this before the wedding. He must've been waffling between me and Sheila until the very last minute. Idiot.

"It was for the best," I say in my best professional voice.

I hang up a few moments later, a sinking feeling sucking all the good ice-cream mojo out of me. I take a deep breath and call the next client on the list.

More of the same. Every client says they'd stick with me if I could match or better Endeavor's discount. I can't. I'd be out of business within three months. Endeavor Media is large enough to take a loss to win more clients in the long run.

Looks like I'm starting from scratch, or looking for a new job at an established agency. Maybe Endeavor Media is hiring and I can burn the place to the ground. Kidding.

I call my lawyer, Bob, to see if I can sue Dave for stealing all my clients.

"I'm sorry, Rowan, your partnership contract didn't have any provision prohibiting either of you from taking clients once your employer relationship ends."

"Why didn't you put it in there?"

"You said it wasn't necessary. You were getting married. If you'd gone through with the marriage, we could've split your assets equitably, but you didn't. I'm sorry I don't have better news. The good news is, Dave signed the papers dissolving your business partnership right away, so that's settled."

"Great."

I get off the phone and debate going for more ice cream. If ever a day called for a double ice-cream snack, it's today. But then I look down to find Felix winding around my leg.

I pick him up and take him to the sofa, where we indulge in a nap together. Sometimes you just need the unconditional love of a pet.

Cooper comes through for me again, showing up with a borrowed truck on Saturday morning and driving me to my apartment in the city. He's kinda like a knight in shining armor, if I believed in that kind of thing.

When we get there, Finn's waiting on the sidewalk.

Rumpled and tired but he's there. Ten thirty in the morning is early for a college student. He resembles Cooper, except Finn has blue eyes and Cooper has brown.

Cooper makes the introductions. Finn offers his hand, and I shake it. "Nice to meet you, Rowan."

"You too. Thanks so much for helping out."

"Of course."

I lead the way to the apartment, thinking I should thank Hailey for raising such great kids. I'm sure their Dad is awesome too. He has to be.

Dave greets us at the door with a guy I've never seen before. "As soon as you finish, he'll be changing the locks, so be quick about it."

"It takes how long it takes," I say, breezing by him.

"Asshole," Cooper says.

I hear a scuffle and look behind me to find Cooper has Dave's arm twisted behind his back. "Try me," Cooper growls.

"I'll press charges if you hurt me!" Dave cries.

"You shoved me first," Cooper says. "Maybe I'll press charges."

"Cooper, please," I say. "Let's just get this done and get out of here."

Cooper releases Dave and glares at him. Dave rubs his arm.

Thankfully, Dave's smart enough to stay out of the way while we get to work. An hour later, my stuff's in the truck. I leave without a goodbye. Dave doesn't deserve one.

"Anything else I can help you with?" Finn asks.

So sweet. "That's all. Finn, it was so nice of you to help out. I really appreciate it."

"No problem," he says. "I thought it was going to be an all-day project. Only took an hour."

My heart squeezes. He was willing to spend his entire Saturday helping out a stranger just because his brother asked him to. "I wish I could pay you. Just know you have my thanks, and anytime you need something I can help with, let me know. I know the ad world, if that helps."

He smiles. "All good."

Cooper gives him a manly half hug, half pat on the back. "Thanks, bro. I'll see you at Sunday family dinner tomorrow." He turns to me. "You're invited too."

My hand goes to my heart. "Me? But I'm not family."

"You should go," Finn says. "Dad's a great cook. Like gourmet level."

"Well, it's not like I'll be having gourmet food any time soon."

"That's the spirit," Cooper says with a wink.

"Sorry, I'd love to go."

"Later!" Finn takes off at a jog.

I turn to Cooper. "Is he going to run back to campus?" He goes to NYU, which is a half-hour subway ride from here.

"Probably. Ready to go?"

"Yeah."

We get into the truck. Cooper starts it and pulls slowly down the street. I take one last look at the apartment I lived in for nearly two years and sigh. In thirty days, more or less, I'll be back in the city. Hopefully, I can find an apartment in my price range. If only they had Clover Park prices here. Of course, there's a reason rent's so high here; it's an awesome, exciting place to live. I'm sure I'll feel that excitement again in time. It's just Dave that's bringing me down.

"You doing okay?" Cooper asks.

"Yeah. It's a relief to have some of my stuff back at least."

"Harper has a she-shed in the backyard where we can store it temporarily."

"A she-shed?"

"Yeah, like a man cave but for women. She converted the garage. It has power, heat, and air conditioning. She uses it like a home office, but she says there's room for your stuff too. She just has a desk in there and a chair."

Apparently, Cooper's been talking to Harper for me. I'm a

little embarrassed he's advocating on my behalf. I can speak up for myself.

"Next time, let me handle talking to people about my stuff, okay?" I say.

"Sure. It just came up. She's my cousin, and we talk regularly."

"Well, I hate to mess with her home office. She's already done so much for me, welcoming me into her home." Mackenzie and Harper were enthusiastic about me staying on longer. Their easy acceptance is strange to me. A good strange, though.

"Not everything is transactional. She's fine with it."

I consider that. I'm used to a transactional relationship. You listen to me; I'll listen to you. You get me lunch; I'll get you lunch. It's basically how I was raised. "I guess so."

"Sometimes it's enough just to be you."

It's never enough. I keep that to myself. No need to unload on Cooper yet again.

We're quiet for a bit as we leave the city and get on the expressway back toward home. I mean my temporary home. Have to remember that.

"Anything you need, just ask," Cooper says. "If I can't help you, I know someone who can."

Why? I nearly blurt.

"Thank you."

"Stop by Happy Endings tonight. I'm working, so I can get you drinks on the house. Dinner too."

I shake my head. "You're stealing from your employer."

"I am my employer."

"You own the place?"

He glances over at me. "I'm not partner yet, but I will be when Dad thinks I'm ready. I've worked my way up since high school. I've been a busboy, waiter, host, kitchen assistant, and now I'm bartender and manager."

He's more put together than most guys in their twenties. Maybe because he's grounded with deep roots in town, a job he loves and can keep for the rest of his life, and close family.

I'd love to have the same, especially a close family. Just not in the cards for me.

"What about Finn and Mackenzie?" I ask. "Do they get to be partners too?"

"Finn could join us if he wants, but I doubt it. He's real creative. He might do something with writing. He won some contests for poetry in high school."

"A sensitive soul. That's nice. Though you don't hear about many poet jobs nowadays."

"Yeah, we'll see. He's always welcome. Mackenzie has her own company. Mom secretly hopes that Mackenzie will one day take over her wedding planning business. Don't mention it to Mackenzie. She's not big on love at the moment."

"Totally understand." I shift toward him, admiring his profile, the sharp lines of his cheekbones and jaw. I face front, warmth rushing through my body. He's gorgeous. My body seems to be on board, even if my head and heart know better. We're close enough for me to breathe in his delicious woodsy scent.

This is not good.

I try to focus on our conversation. "So being manager means you can have as much food and drink as you want on the house?"

"Being the owner's son means I can have all the free food and drink I want. If it makes you feel better, I'll pay for your stuff, but then it sounds more like a date. You okay with that?"

He glances over at me.

Adrenaline surges through me. *Danger! Danger!* No dating, no men. Not even sweet, sexy, gorgeous men who're there for you at every turn. Oh no. I'm way too into this guy.

I break into a cold sweat. I'd bolt, but we're stuck in the confines of a truck cab together. Not a great idea to jump out the door as we speed past the Bronx.

"You okay?" he asks.

I rub the side of my neck. "Dating is off the table. Nothing personal. Just, ya know, heartbroken and devastated. I thought I was going to be married a week ago."

"No problem. I don't know why I said that. Friends?"

"Yes, of course. Friends. Thank you for understanding."

He reaches over and gives my hand a squeeze. A zing of sensation races up my arm.

I rub my arm. "In thirty days I'll have my condo deposit back, and I'll be moving back to the city. I want my old life back."

"Sorry to say, your old life is gone. Didn't you say all your clients went to Dave's cousin's agency?"

"Yes, and I can't afford to lure them back, but I can get new clients. Eventually." I exhale sharply. "To tell you the truth, I went into advertising following in my mom's footsteps. Somehow I thought it would make me feel closer to her, understand the life she led before she died. But it's a different world now than when she worked in it."

"Do you like that kind of work?"

"Parts of it." I rub my temple. "The thought of starting from scratch just makes me tired. Maybe advertising isn't what I'm meant to do."

"If there was ever a time for a fresh start, this is it. Give it time and think about what you want. Whatever you decide, I'll be here."

I cross my arms, hugging myself. Did I meet the perfect guy? Is the universe making up for the devastation Dave wrought? This can't be real. Cooper's just too good to be true.

The next day, I stand with Mackenzie on the front porch of her parents' house, a two-story colonial-style home with natural-colored wood siding and brown shutters. She rings the bell. Mackenzie's holding a bottle of wine, which she says is mandatory to deal with her mom's constant matchmaking.

"Welcome, come in," Hailey says, answering the door in a

pink jumpsuit and heels. She looks like a fashion model. "So glad you could come too, Rowan."

"Thank you for inviting me."

Looking at Hailey, I feel way underdressed. Mackenzie told me it was casual, so I'm wearing a long-sleeve V-neck cotton shirt with jeans. Mackenzie's wearing a light sweater and jeans with boots. Come to think of it, she does look really put together.

"Oh, my favorite wine," Hailey says to Mackenzie, taking it from her. "Thank you."

She leads the way inside.

"Hey, Rowan," Finn says, joining us.

"Hey, good to see you again."

Mackenzie gives him a hug. "How's college?"

"Busy. Getting ready for midterms."

"Ohh, I don't miss exams," Mackenzie says.

"Have a seat," Hailey says, indicating a sectional sofa in the living room. "What can I get you to drink?"

"Wine," Mackenzie says.

"Same, please," I say.

"Where's Dad?" Mackenzie asks.

"Out back with Cooper," Finn answers. "They're cooking ribs, which is, like, a whole-day thing."

Hailey flutters a hand in the air. "I told him he didn't have to make such an elaborate recipe. He started marinating yesterday. He says everyone likes ribs, so it's worth it. Is that okay with you, Rowan?"

"Of course."

She nods once and hurries into the kitchen.

I join Mackenzie and Finn on the sofa, anxiously waiting for Cooper to walk in. I don't know why I'm on the edge of my seat. Yesterday, after we moved my furniture into Harper's she-shed with her help, he took me out for ice cream again. But that was just because I needed a pick-me-up. It wasn't a date. I mean, really, given my circumstances, how can I be expected to resist the best ice cream in the state?

"I thought tonight was casual," I say to Mackenzie under my breath. "I feel underdressed compared to your mom."

"Oh, no, that's just her wardrobe," Mackenzie says. "The only time she wears casual clothes is when she's cleaning or gardening. You should've seen how she dressed me when I was little."

"At least you looked like a mini-Mom fashion plate," Finn says. "She dressed me and Cooper in matching outfits like we were twins, even though we're four years apart. We looked ridiculous."

"You looked cute," Mackenzie says. "Cooper looked ridiculous because he was older."

Finn laughs. "Yeah."

"I'd love to see pictures," I say.

Mackenzie gestures toward the stairs. "Check out the photo gallery on the stairway. Some classic Finn-Cooper twin action going on there."

I head over. Oh my God, they're adorable. Cooper looks disgruntled in one, but is mostly smiling widely for the camera. Such a cutie. Finn's cute as a button too. My favorite is when Cooper has his arm around Finn's shoulders. They look so proud to be brothers. My eyes water, loving that bond. I always wished for a sibling I could bond with.

Cooper appears, smiling at me. My pulse spikes. It's bizarre the reaction I have to him. First of all, I'm not ready for a relationship of any kind. Second, I'm not staying in town long. Third, he's *amazing*. No denying it. Gorgeous, sweet, sexy. If the circumstances were different…

"I see you found the wall of fame," he says. "For the full picture, you'll need to look in my room. Some highlights—the blue ribbon I got for swim team in fourth grade and three rec basketball trophies from middle school. Unfortunately, our high school team never made it to the championship."

I laugh. "I'm sure it's a shrine to the greatness of Cooper Campbell."

"As it should be. Mom turned Mackenzie's room into an

exercise room since she left home first. My and Finn's rooms remain just as we left them."

"Didn't your parents want a guest room?"

"They just let guests sleep in a teen-boy guest room."

"Ah."

"Dinner will be ready in a couple of minutes. Come on." He offers me his arm.

I stare at his arm, but don't take it. "I don't want your parents to get the wrong idea about us."

"Mom knows your deal," he says. "Dad's the one who taught me to be a gentleman. His dad insisted on it with him and his brothers after his dad's mom was treated poorly by her husband. Her second marriage was to a man who had gentleman manners, and that's all it took to start a legendary family tradition."

"So if I don't take your arm, your dad will be mad at you?"

"Exactly."

"Hmmm…"

"You can walk in on my arm," Finn calls from the living room.

"She barely knows you," Cooper says, walking over to argue with his brother.

I walk into the dining room with Mackenzie. We share a smile. It's sweet but unnecessary to have an escort into the dining room.

Cooper's dad, Josh, sets a platter of ribs on the table. "Hope you're hungry, Rowan."

"I am. Thanks for having me."

"Course." He walks around the table and offers his hand to me. Like Cooper, he has brown hair and warm brown eyes, which crinkle at the corners when he smiles. "I'm Josh. Seems you met everyone in the family except me. Sorry you're going through a rough patch. You've landed in a good spot."

I shake his hand. "Thanks. I feel fortunate. Your kids are wonderful. They've all been so helpful."

His chest puffs out. "That's how we raised 'em."

Mackenzie hugs him. "How's your tennis elbow?"

"Bah, fine. I'm doing my exercises." He turns to me. "I don't even play tennis."

Mackenzie squeezes his arm. "It's from yard work."

Hailey hustles in with side dishes and gestures to Mackenzie with her head. Mackenzie goes to the kitchen and brings in extra napkins and more side dishes. There's corn bread, green beans with almonds, coleslaw, baked beans, and fries.

My stomach growls.

Cooper takes the seat next to me. "Someone's hungry."

I press a hand to my stomach. "Everything looks so good."

"The fries are from Happy Endings," Hailey says.

"So's everything else," Josh says.

"Not true," Hailey protests. "I made the coleslaw, and you made the ribs." She lifts the rib platter and passes it to me first. "Take what you like and pass it along."

The passing of plates works like clockwork around the table. I take a little bit of everything.

"Do you often have a big Sunday family dinner?" I ask.

"Every Sunday," Cooper says. "We don't all make it every Sunday, but we try."

Everyone starts to eat. I try to be neat with my ribs, but the sauce makes it impossible. After a while I just give up and go for it. Seems like that's what everyone's doing anyway, even Hailey, who always looks so put together.

Conversation revolves around Hailey checking in with each of her kids. They don't seem to mind her questions, and everyone laughs a lot. It's wonderful.

After dinner, Hailey brings out homemade apple pie with whipped cream.

"Dad made the pie and whipped cream from scratch," Finn tells me. "You have to try it."

I put a hand on my stomach. "Someone should've warned me. I'm so full."

"You can take some home with you," Hailey says. "It's good for breakfast too."

"True," Josh says.

"Dad's taken a bunch of cooking classes," Cooper says. "He's the gourmet in this family."

"Helps at the restaurant," Josh says. "You should take some too, Coop."

"That's what the chef is for," Cooper says.

"It helps with menu planning," Josh says.

Cooper clamps his mouth shut. I have a feeling they've had this conversation before.

Hailey guides the conversation to the latest at her work, where she's landed a big client recently. A young senator with presidential aspirations.

"Have you been showing Rowan around?" Hailey asks Mackenzie and Cooper.

"I introduced her to Felix," Mackenzie says. "I think he likes her better than me."

"He's a great cat," I say.

"I introduced Rowan to the wonder of Shane's Scoops," Cooper says.

"Amazing ice cream," I say. "I'm in heaven. Highlight of my day."

Hailey smiles. "Agree. Their reputation is well-earned. Rowan, Cooper's told me a bit about your situation, and I wanted to let you know you're welcome to stay with us for as long as you like. We have two empty bedrooms. Plenty of space."

"Absolutely," Josh says.

"She's already at my place," Mackenzie says. "I have dibs. We told her she could stay for the next month while she waits to get her condo deposit back."

"Oh. I didn't know," Hailey says with a sunny smile. "Glad to hear it." Then she says to Mackenzie in a low voice, "If you'd let me know what's going on in your life, I'd appreciate it."

"I just told you," Mackenzie says.

I smile. "Thank you for the offer, Hailey."

Everyone goes back to eating in comfortable silence.

Hailey has a wonderful caring motherly feel about her. I noticed it when she was my wedding planner, and now that I'm enjoying family dinner, I find myself wanting to be part of this lovely family.

"My place is also a possibility," Cooper says, breaking the silence.

"That's off the table," Josh says.

"Why?" Cooper asks.

"You seriously have to ask why?" Josh says. "You have a one bedroom."

"I'd give her my bed and take the sofa," Cooper says.

"Stop," Josh says.

Cooper frowns.

"That's very nice of you to offer," I tell Cooper.

He grunts, giving his dad side-eye. Josh shakes his head.

"Mackenzie's place would be more fun for Rowan," Finn says. Cooper looks insulted.

Josh puts his elbow on the table. "Arm-wrestle you for her, Cooper."

My eyes widen. *Is he serious?*

"Dad! You have tennis elbow. I'm not going to arm-wrestle you."

"That's my other elbow," Josh says.

Cooper lines up his arm next to his dad's, and they start to arm-wrestle. I watch in fascination. They seem to be evenly matched. Finn and Mackenzie start cheering. Finn for Cooper; Mackenzie for Josh.

"What's that, Rowan?" Josh asks.

Cooper turns to look at me, and Josh slams Cooper's arm to the table.

"Ha!" Josh says.

"Sneaky," Cooper mutters.

Josh and Hailey exchange knowing looks. I hope they don't think something's going on with me and Cooper. That would look especially bad to Hailey, who saw me totally in love with Dave not long ago. Foolish me.

After dessert, Mackenzie, Finn, and Cooper clear the dishes immediately. I jump up to help.

Once we're in the kitchen, Mackenzie leans close to whisper, "Sorry my family's so weird."

"They're awesome."

Hailey pokes her head in the kitchen. "Rowan, you're a guest. No need to do cleanup. Come on out to the living room. I'd like to talk to you."

"Sure."

I glance back over my shoulder. Cooper smiles like he knows what it's about. Mackenzie shoos me out. Josh passes me on his way outside to clean the grill and gives me a smile.

I step into the living room. Does everyone in this family know what this is about except me?

Hailey gestures for me to have a seat. After I do, she says, "I know you're getting back on your feet with your ad agency. In the meantime, I wondered if you'd like to work with me as my assistant. My longtime business partner, Ally, recently left to pursue her dream of becoming a romance novelist."

My jaw gapes. "You want me to help you with wedding planning?" Does she not remember that I was just dumped at my wedding eight days ago? (But who's counting?)

She nods and smiles.

"I don't know. All those happy brides…"

"There's a lot to the business side too. Marketing and advertising, doing the books, logistics, strategy. It's not just gowns and flowers. This would be just to hold you over while you rebuild. We can even do part time if you like. I'm flexible."

"Can I think about it?"

"Of course. I promise I'm a good boss."

"I'm sure you are. I enjoyed working with you for my own wedding."

"Now you can see under the hood for how the whole machine works. Confession: it's mostly powered by sheer grit, which I know you have an abundance of. Just look at you, already working to put the pieces of your life back together. Some women would still be glued to the sofa, watching TV and stuffing themselves with cookies."

"That would've been easier. Though Cooper's been tempting me with ice cream."

"Ice cream's good for you. It has calcium and protein. And it's a known mood booster."

"Really?"

"I haven't found anyone who thought differently."

We laugh.

"You have a lovely family," I say. "I don't think I'd be in as good a shape as I am without them."

"Thank you. I hope you'll join us for another dinner. Open invitation, every Sunday."

"I would love that."

She beams a sunny smile. "Good. You're exactly the kind of person I want for…my children. My grown children."

I cock my head. For a moment there, I thought she was going to say for Cooper. "Thanks."

"Cooper's a lot like his dad, laid-back, easygoing, but you'll find underneath that, there's a spine of steel. He won't ever let you down. Just between you and me, he's never been a player. He's had a few relationships—"

"Mom."

She whirls to face Cooper. "Are you finished in the kitchen?"

"Yes. Were you talking about me?" He glances at me, pink creeping up his neck.

I bite back a smile.

She smiles serenely. "Just saying how you take after your dad."

"He's much trickier than me. Did you see him psych me out to win arm wrestling?"

Hailey gives me a knowing look. "I did."

He turns to me. "If you want, I can walk you home."

"Oh. Mackenzie drove me."

"I'm staying here for a while," Mackenzie calls from the kitchen. She steps into the living room. "It's okay if you want to head home, or you can stay. Dad and I are watching football."

The one advantage to being Dave-free is not having sports on all the time. I turn to Cooper. "You don't want to watch the game?"

"Nah. I prefer to play than watch, though I'll go in person if someone has tickets."

"I think I'll go now, then. Thanks for a lovely dinner."

I say my goodbyes to everyone. Hailey surprises me with a hug goodbye.

I leave with a smile on my face.

6

———

Cooper

Rowan fit right in with my family. Another point in her favor. The more time I spend with her, the more I like her. *Remember Brianna. She pulled the rug right out from under you after you helped her get back on her feet.*

Rowan looks up at me. "So it's pretty safe to walk in the dark here?"

"Absolutely. People don't even lock their doors half the time. And the key's usually under the mat or in a nearby frog planter. Sometimes it's a turtle."

She laughs. "Grandmom used to keep a key in a fake rock."

"Did you grow up in a small town too?"

"Actually, it was more like the country. She lived on a farm in Pennsylvania. After Grandpop died, the farm shut down. It was miles to the neighbor's house. I got very good at speed bicycling."

"Speed bicycling sounds awesome."

"It is. Nothing like the wind in your hair. I always took my helmet off when I got out of sight of the house."

"Naughty girl."

She smiles. "For the most part, I was the perfect straight A, rule-following granddaughter."

"The bike brought out your bad-girl side. I bet you'd love to ride a motorcycle."

"Too dangerous." She glances around. "Good thing you're walking me because I don't remember how we got to your parents' house."

"It's a grid, not too hard. Look up a map of town and you'll get it in no time. If you ever get lost, head that way toward Main Street." I gesture toward it. "All roads lead to Main Street. Mackenzie's house is on Catoonah Street just off Main."

"Got it. Your family's so nice. I envy you coming from such a close-knit family."

"You're the first woman I've brought home to meet my parents."

"Really? Your mom said you've had multiple relationships."

"I knew she was talking about me! Don't listen to her."

"Why? Is it not true?"

"No, it's true I've had relationships. I just prefer you get information about me directly from the source."

"And you never invited anyone home to meet your parents?"

"Well, I did invite my last girlfriend, Brianna. She went to the beach with friends and texted me from there that she wouldn't be coming. Mom always thought she was too flighty. Guess she was right since after I helped Brianna get back on her feet, she moved on."

"So I really am the first woman at Sunday dinner."

"Yeah, and it was dicey because not only is Mom a wedding planner, she's an intense matchmaker. That's mostly why I don't bring anyone home. I don't want her to pounce, asking about the relationship, where it's going, you know. All that love and commitment stuff. She means well."

"I guess it was different since I was with Mackenzie."

"Yeah, I seem to have gotten off-track. I was just making a joke about meeting the parents. It flopped."

She smiles and elbows me. "Does she embarrass you with

stories of when you were a kid? Mackenzie and Harper already told me you used to run wild and throw food at them."

I laugh. "Yeah, well, that's true. Just in good fun. They threw food back too. I bet they left that part out."

"They did."

We walk in companionable silence for a bit. She takes a deep breath and stops to stare at the sky. "You can see so many stars here."

"Yeah. The city has too much light pollution, and all those skyscrapers block the view."

"It's beautiful."

She takes a picture with her phone and checks it. "It didn't really capture it."

"Yeah, it's better just to take it in with your own eyes." She starts walking again, and I keep up. "You should take that job with my mom."

"I'm seriously considering it. I mean, I can't afford to be picky. I just don't know if I can handle all those happy-in-love couples."

"Think of it as being an event planner."

"She did say she'd be flexible with me working part-time hours."

"There you go. I'd hire you to be a waitress at Happy Endings, but we're fully staffed."

"Oh God, no. I was a waitress one summer in college, and I was terrible at it. Kept getting the orders wrong and dropping dishes. Not for me."

"It would be cool if you stuck around." The words are out of my mouth before I can stop them. Shit. Back it up.

Her eyes widen, and she shifts, putting some distance between us.

I hold a palm up. "No pressure. Just thought—"

"I just ended a serious relationship."

"I know that's not easy. I ended one last year."

"You did?"

"Yeah. Brianna. She moved to the city and ghosted me."

"I sound just like her. Someone you helped who wants to move to the city."

"You'd never ghost me."

"No, I wouldn't," she says softly. "How do you know that?"

"I watched you with my family. You liked us. And the feeling was mutual. Anyone who can handle a Campbell Sunday dinner is my kind of people. And my kind would never bail without a goodbye."

Our hands brush as we walk, sending a jolt through me. I like her. I know I should keep my distance. I don't think she'd ghost me, but I do think she'll leave as soon as she can to start a new life in the city. I can only take the city in small doses. My life is here.

I shift away so our hands don't accidentally touch. "Anyway, you should take the job. You'll feel better having some money in the bank while you rebuild your business."

"And that's the only reason you want me to take the job?"

"You'd really be helping Mom out. She's back to a one-woman operation. She often says she wishes she could clone herself."

"Mackenzie would be the closest thing you could get to a clone."

"Well, I wouldn't go that far. Mackenzie's far more pragmatic and not so into the fairy-tale wedding Mom helps brides achieve. Mom never pressured her, just offered an open invitation, which Mackenzie didn't take her up on."

She's quiet. I can feel her staring at me. There's definitely chemistry between us. I've felt it every time we touch. *Resist. Stay strong.*

I turn to her and meet her gaze. She looks away fast. "You can walk to most places in town, but you might want a car for grocery shopping, errands, or getting to the train station. Most big stores are a half hour away."

"Car, insurance, gas. That sounds expensive."

"I'm close with my cousin Mason, who works at Exotic and Classic Restorations. That's who I borrowed a truck from to move your stuff. I'm sure he could find you something to get around in that's not too expensive."

"That name sounds familiar. Exotic and Classic Restorations. Is that the shop in Eastman, Connecticut, on the TV show *Hot Finds*?"

"That's the one. You a fan?"

"I've seen it. Dave used to watch it. His dream was to own a classic car once he got a second home in the country. Now he has a llama farm with Sheila, so I guess he's on his way."

"Of all things, a llama farm."

"I don't want to talk about it. Back to *Hot Finds*. I've seen Mason on the show with Parker and Ty."

"That's right. My cousin and uncles do the show together. Course, it's not as exciting as my aunt. Claire Jordan is a household name."

"Harper told me that's her mom. What's she like?"

"She's just a regular person."

"Harper doesn't look like her."

"Those Campbell genes. My uncle Jake is the identical twin of my dad, so the kids in both families look like siblings."

"Identical twins sounds so fun. I used to wish for an identical twin. Do they run in your family?"

"Well, I'm not sure if that's genetic, but there is another set of identical twins. Mason's younger brothers."

"Do the twins ever switch places and fool people?"

I launch into a family classic. The story of how my uncle Jake and my dad, Josh, switched places. Jake took out Claire, who was expecting Dad. The whole reason was because Dad wanted to take out Mom and prove that she only wanted men with money. Which wasn't true. That launched an all-out frenemy war between Dad and Mom that's legend in town.

I finish the story just as we reach the front walk of her house. She's in high spirits, delighting in the war between my parents, who now look like the perfect loving couple. We arrive at the front porch of Mackenzie and Harper's house.

"I just love it," she says. "You'd never know."

"I'm sure you'll hear about it eventually. It's a favorite story both in our family and in town."

"Is your mom embarrassed about it?"

"She tries to shut it down because she thinks it doesn't look good for her wedding planning business. She should've thought of that before she engaged in war."

She shakes her head. "She must've been so mad at him. Some of the stuff she did!"

"The funny part is, he thought they were just playing around."

She meets my eyes, getting serious. A tension fills the air between us. I don't move a muscle.

"I might take the job," she says.

"Great."

"Goodnight." She leans forward just as I shift, her lips meeting mine. A rush of lust goes through me on contact.

She slaps a hand over her mouth. "I meant to kiss you on the cheek, but you moved."

I lean down and kiss her cheek. She places her hand on my cheek, drawing me in for a real kiss. *Yesss.* I keep it gentle even as lust surges through my veins.

She leans back, her fingers on her lips, her blue eyes huge.

My lips curve up. "Goodnight."

I head home, energy coursing through my limbs. I want to pump my fist in the air, but have to satisfy myself with an internal cheer. I knew there was something there.

I glance over my shoulder and catch her watching me go. I lift a hand in farewell, and she hurries to the front door.

I smile to myself and jog the rest of the way home. As long as I keep it light and casual, it'll be okay. She's a flight risk.

Part of me wants to fly with her.

7

———————

Rowan

I took the job. And, no, this has nothing to do with Cooper or that kiss, which can never happen again. It has to do with not being a fool. I need money, and I've had a flexible job handed to me by a woman I admire. And I'm not the kind of person who can just sit around waiting for things to happen. I'm always go, go, go.

Okay, and Cooper's family sort of sucked me in. They're just so lovely and close. I want to feel part of that for a little longer. I've never had that.

"You can go at noon," Hailey says to me. "I know I threw a lot at you today." We're in her office, where she just explained her organizational software and how she tracks invoices. Her office is just as beautiful and put together as she is. Her organization is immaculate in built-in bookcases and storage cubbies. Antique pieces, landscape paintings, and a vase of fresh flowers make it feel homey.

I'm sitting at Ally's old desk. "Actually, I'd like to work full time. You can pay me for part-time, no problem. I'm not good with just sitting around."

"Don't you want to work on getting your own business back in order?"

"Welp, I lost my clients, so it'll take a while to find new

clients. And the truth is, I'm not sure if I want to open another ad agency. It was a career I jumped into because it's what my mom did. Maybe this is a good time to reassess, you know?"

"Absolutely. I'd love to have you, though I would of course pay you for your hours."

"Are you sure?"

"Yes. Ally was full time until a month ago. I just thought you'd want time for your own thing. We'll play it by ear, okay? Any time you need off, just let me know."

"Great, thank you."

"Sure. I usually have lunch here I've packed from home. There's some leftover chicken francaise and salad in the refrigerator from our last wedding, which you're welcome to. Or if you want to pick up something across the street at Happy Endings, just tell Josh I sent you. Oh, wait, it's Cooper on Mondays. Tell him I sent you, and he'll give you a meal on the house."

I flush just hearing his name. Cooper kissed me last night. Or I kissed him. I'm not sure who moved first but wow. That kiss was nothing like I've felt before. It was a shock to the system and at the same time warm and languid, like I could just fall into it over and over.

What was I thinking?

You weren't thinking. That was all feeling.

I put a hand to my warm cheek.

"Rowan, are you okay?"

I drop my hand, embarrassed. "Yes, sorry. Wedding leftovers sound good for lunch. I don't want to keep mooching free food off your family's restaurant."

"We're happy to help."

I nod. "I need to stand on my own two feet as soon as possible."

"Would you like an advance on your paycheck?"

I hold up a palm. "You're far too generous. I'll earn my keep. You can pay me after I do the work. Besides, you don't even know if I'm a good fit yet."

She smiles, her blue eyes sparkling like she has a secret. "I already know you're a great fit. I'm so glad you're here. Let's go grab lunch in the back."

I follow her to the kitchen, and I'm instantly reminded of being here with Cooper, eating delicious leftover cake with a champagne chaser, all the while being enthralled by his warmth and charm. By all rights I should've been a complete mess at the time, yet I was comfortable enough to open up to him and share about my complicated family situation.

Being back at Ludbury House hasn't been as difficult as I feared because it's colored by memories of being here with Cooper. It's like his presence made my disaster of a wedding fade into the background. Not completely, but enough for me to cope.

While we eat lunch, Hailey tells me the schedule for the rest of the day. There's two new client consultations, and then she wants to show me the accounting system so I can start adding invoices to it. She's gotten behind on that.

She finishes her lunch before me, peeks in the refrigerator, and turns to me. "I thought I had two bottles of champagne in here, but there's only one. Would you mind running across the street and asking Cooper for another bottle? It needs to be chilled. I always offer new clients champagne to get off on the right foot. We've got two new clients coming this afternoon."

I choke on my lunch, coughing profusely. I grab my water and take a quick drink.

"Are you okay?" she asks.

I nod through watery eyes.

"I'd do it, but I like to do a meditation session before meeting a new client. Helps me get into a Zen state."

"Yes, of course." I am the assistant, after all. Time to assist. It's just that I'd hoped not to run into Cooper for at least a week. Then enough time would've passed for us both to pretend that kiss never happened.

I push back from the table.

She holds up a palm. "You can finish your lunch. It's not that much of a rush."

My appetite deserted me when nerves took over. "I like to check things off the list as soon as they land on it."

"That's good to know. I'll have to be careful when I ask you to do something. From now on, I'll wait until you finish your lunch."

I nod once and clear my dishes, putting the plate, silverware, and my glass in the dishwasher like I saw Cooper do the last time we were here. Cooper with the warm brown eyes, the scruffy jaw, killer smile. Not to mention the bod—

His mom interrupts my dangerous line of thought. "Oh, remind Cooper the kids are stopping by on Saturday to paint the windows for Halloween. It's a town tradition where the kids from the middle school paint spooky scenes on the shop windows on Main Street. It's temporary paint. They'll come by again in December to paint a winter scene."

"No problem." I head for the door.

"You're just the kind of woman I'd pick for him."

I stop and slowly turn around. "Excuse me?"

She waves that away. "Not that I have any say in my children's love lives. But you would be a good balance. Type A to type B. Not to mention, you're kind and smart, and you have grit."

"You got all that from planning my wedding and working with me for one day?"

"I got all that at our first consultation. I can read people. That's what makes me such a good wedding planner. I anticipate people's needs and match them."

"Cooper mentioned you were a matchmaker."

She tosses her long strawberry blond hair over one shoulder. "Yes, well, I guess my reputation precedes me. I love love. Obviously, or I wouldn't run Love Junkies. Did you know we also offer sologamy ceremonies? That's marrying yourself. It's all about self-love and empowerment. Ally started that service years ago, and it's continued to this day."

My mind is about to explode. I don't know if I should focus more on the odd concept of marrying myself or the fact that she's trying to match me with Cooper. Definitely that last thing.

"Cooper's a great guy—" I start.

"I'm glad you see it too."

"But I can't get involved with him or anyone. It was only nine days ago I thought I was going to marry someone else."

She sighs. "Love can be so inconvenient. Trust me, I know. I never thought I'd fall madly in love with Josh, especially after he baited me night and day. The man was a beast."

I can't help my smile. "Cooper told me. The legendary frenemy war."

She huffs. "Off with you. I can't believe people are still telling that silly story about me and Josh. It's old news."

"Not to me." I walk off, smiling to myself.

Cooper

I'm slicing limes at the bar at the beginning of what promises to be another long, dull Monday shift when *she* walks in. I haven't been able to get Rowan out of my mind. I went to bed thinking about her and that kiss. Woke up thinking about her too, in a much more carnal way. Took care of that in the shower.

I smile. "Hi."

"Hi." Her voice comes out high. Classic sign of distress in a woman. Her cheeks are flushed pink too. I'm not the only one thinking about that kiss.

"What can I get you?"

She speaks in a rush. "Your mom needs a bottle of chilled champagne, and don't forget about the kids coming on Saturday to paint the windows for Halloween."

I smile. "Sounds like you took the job."

"Yes. And I'm doing it full-time until I can figure out my next steps. Not because of you." Her hands flutter in the air. "I mean, not that you said that." She puts her hands down and lifts her cute chin. "It's because I'm not sure I want to do advertising anymore."

I lean down to the wine refrigerator and pull out a bottle of champagne. I always keep the kind Mom wants for clients chilling here. "It's good to take some time to consider your options."

I straighten to find her leaning over the bar to look at me. She jerks back.

"Options," she echoes, her eyes locked on mine.

"Yeah." I'm not sure if she's extremely attracted to me or freaking out about that kiss. Maybe I should say something about it. Calm her nerves.

I hand her the champagne bottle. "Last night—"

"Is this the right kind?" She examines the label. "Hailey's particular for her clients."

"Trust me, it's the right stuff. We're her supplier. Rowan, I just want—"

"Thank you!" She does an about-face and practically sprints from the bar.

I may need to do damage control.

Rowan

Everything's cool, everything's cool. I was professional and did my job exactly as instructed. Was I flushed with heat just looking at him? That doesn't matter. Did he notice? Doesn't matter. I can say it was from the exertion of jogging across the street. Which will only come up if I have to talk to him again, which I don't have to. Not really. Unless Hailey sends me on another errand.

Was this her matchmaking?

I hurry across the street. No, it couldn't be. I saw for myself there was only one bottle of champagne in the refrigerator at Ludbury House.

Why is my heart racing? I'm not that out of shape.

I make it to the front porch of Ludbury House and take

several deep breaths, trying desperately to find my own Zen. I've always sucked at meditation and breathing exercises. I can't sit still and do nothing and especially can't empty my mind of thoughts. My mind is always whirling, what's next, what do I need to do, what about tonight and tomorrow, plan, plan, plan.

I step inside and see Hailey's office door is closed. She's probably doing her meditation. I put the champagne in the refrigerator and open the freezer, letting the cold air help me chill.

I didn't want it to be awkward with Cooper. He brought up last night, and I completely lost my cool. It's too soon to get involved with someone, and once I get my life back together, I'm heading back to the city. I'm not cut out for small-town life. Everyone moves slower here, and there's just way too much friendliness with complete strangers. Like me. I'm the complete stranger.

I know I'm lucky I landed here. Lucky I met Cooper in the first place. That doesn't mean I'm staying. I'm not about to change my life plan for a guy. Not even one who's gorgeous and a good kisser. My breath comes harder.

Okay, I'm officially freaking out.

Hailey pops out of her office. "We're meeting with Alexis and Lenny in ten. Follow me. I'll show you how I do setup." She carries two large binders and leads the way toward the back of Ludbury House.

I follow. "I got the champagne and reminded Cooper about the Halloween paintings."

"Thank you!"

We reach the ballroom, where wedding receptions are held. It's mostly empty now with a round table near the center. A crystal chandelier sparkles overhead. Hardwood floors, of course. I remember meeting in here for my own wedding consultation a year ago. Dave was agreeable through the whole thing. We probably looked like the perfect wedding couple. Even I believed it.

Hailey takes a seat and gestures for me to sit next to her.

"Take a look through the binder to familiarize yourself with our offerings. I'm going to get the champagne and glasses."

"Sure." I flip through the binder. No prices. Smart. The idea is that you fall in love with an option. Floral centerpieces, floral decorations, corsages, or more simple with artificial flowers and streamers decorating the place. There's definitely an A+ option versus a C. They even offer wedding gown assistance with recommendations to top bridal boutiques, including having an original gown created just for you. I confess I leaned toward the high-end options. I convinced myself it was a once-in-a-lifetime event I'd always remember. For some brides, it would've been.

Hailey returns with the champagne, a towel to open it cleanly, and a plastic corsage box. I remember she was careful not to spill a drop when she opened the champagne for us.

"Hailey, I haven't received the final invoice from you yet for my wedding, but I was wondering if I could pay it down with every paycheck? You wouldn't have to pay me until my debt was cleared."

She smiles kindly. "We'll work something out."

"Okay." I'm not sure what that means.

She checks the time, pinches her cheeks, and rises gracefully from her chair. "I'll be up front to greet them. You stay here and prepare yourself mentally. Whatever the bride wants, she gets."

I nod.

She walks briskly to the front of Ludbury House. A few moments later, a chime rings out. I can hear voices, but not what they're saying.

Hailey appears, all bright smiles, and gestures the bride-to-be, Alexis, and her fiancé, Lenny, in. I'm not one to make snap judgments, but if I were, I'd say this bride is thrilled to plan her wedding, and he just went along to please her. He looks uncomfortable.

"Have a seat," Hailey says, gesturing to the two chairs across from me. "Alexis, Lenny, this is my assistant, Rowan."

"Hi, nice to meet you," I say.

They barely acknowledge me with a slight nod.

Hailey smiles brightly. "I'm so glad to meet you both in person after our emails and call. This is for you, Alexis." She hands her a small pink rose corsage.

"Thank you. How darling!" Alexis pins the corsage to her blouse.

"I'm on my lunch break, so let's move this along," Lenny says.

"Of course," Hailey says smoothly. "Rowan, get them started on the cake selection. That always helps lend itself to theme. Champagne, anyone?"

"Sure," Alexis says.

Lenny nods.

I open the binder to the cake section and turn it toward them. Hailey pops the champagne and pours, setting the glasses in front of the happy couple.

Alexis pushes the binder away. "I already know exactly what I want. An outdoor ceremony and reception here in June."

Hailey makes notes on a small notepad. "We've done many of those. A beautiful option."

Alexis continues enthusiastically, "Ludbury House will be my second ceremony. I'm also having a ceremony for my family at the Episcopalian church in my hometown of Greenport. I want a horse-drawn carriage to take me from the church ceremony to the—"

Lenny rolls his eyes. "I told you that's not practical. Greenport is too far from Clover Park."

"That's what I want."

"That's quite a long ride," Hailey says diplomatically. "It would likely take more than an hour by horse and carriage."

My mind checks out while they argue. I had romantic ideas when I planned my wedding too. I was so excited. Baby's breath with pink roses, silk streamers, a gown out of a fairy tale. All for nothing. Love is an illusion. My throat closes with emotion, and I look away, hoping no one notices the tears stinging my eyes.

Alexis frowns and waves her hand in front of my face. "Hell-oo! Could you do your job and show me the flower options? Geez, I thought this place was supposed to be all about the happy couple."

I blink a few times. "Sorry. I, uh…" I look down at the binder, and it swims before my eyes.

Hailey jumps in and turns to the flower section of the binder. "June is a wonderful time for flowers. We can get anything you want."

They launch into a discussion of flower arrangements while I try to focus. The reminder of my own wedding planning is too fresh. Sweat dots my upper lip. I'm suddenly unbearably hot, a ringing sounding in my ears. Oh shit, am I going to pass out? I need to get out of here, but I can't let Hailey down.

Hailey's hand lands on my arm. "Could you bring me a glass of water? Get yourself one too."

I nod and walk quickly from the room, relieved not to embarrass myself by passing out. I pull my hair up and pull my shirt away from my body with my other hand, trying to cool off.

Once I get to the kitchen, I run my wrists under cold water and use a wet paper towel to pat the back of my neck and my forehead. I pour two glasses of water and guzzle one down. I need to get back. Hailey will think I'm the world's worst assistant if I can't even get through a client consultation. It's only the basis of her entire business.

I return, setting Hailey's water down for her and slipping into my seat.

Hailey checks in with me with her sharp mom vision. "Thanks." She turns to Alexis. "What else have you dreamed of for your special day?"

"A big poufy princess gown with a long train, a large wedding party, and at the end we'll release butterflies in the air."

Lenny bursts out laughing. "Butterflies. Really? And how

much is that going to cost? They're flying around outside for free already. I say keep it simple and cheap."

"Would you like to have a cocktail hour before the meal?" Hailey asks, turning the page in the binder.

Lenny grimaces. "I love ya, babe, but I've got better things to do. Keep it on budget, or we're doing this in Vegas like I wanted to in the first place." He gets up and leaves.

Alexis bursts into tears. My heart lurches. I so feel for her. She's all in; he's not. Next thing you know, you're jilted on your wedding day. Nausea rises in my throat. I look to the ceiling, desperately trying to get myself under control.

Hailey speaks in a soothing tone to Alexis. "Every couple has a bumpy road in the beginning. A wedding can feel very high stakes. I'm here to make it easier for you. Let's get back to the flowers for outdoors. I personally think the roses on the trellis we have would look amazing in wedding pictures, but there are other options."

Alexis looks at the binder and then looks at me. "Your assistant looks sick. I hope it's not contagious."

I focus on breathing, hoping the nausea will pass.

Hailey turns to me. "Rowan, go ahead to my office and lie down for a bit. I'll be in to check on you later."

I get up and leave, wondering what in the world I'm doing here. And why did I sign up for full time?

Since there's no sofa in Hailey's office, I sit in the cushioned office chair and rest my head in my hands, closing my eyes and taking slow, deep breaths. I so don't want to disappoint Hailey by not being available to help. I have to keep an emotional distance between me and the happy brides who come in here. Hailey's running a business here.

An hour later, Hailey walks in and shuts the door behind her. "How're you doing?"

I smile. "Fine. Just needed a breather."

"Look, Rowan, if you need to sit this next one out—"

"I'm fine. I want to help."

"I'm not sure if that's the best idea."

"I want to keep busy. It's good for me."

"Okay, we'll try again, but if you need another breather, just get up and go. I'll understand."

I nod.

The chime rings. She turns toward the door. "They're early. Ready?"

"Ready."

I hurry back to the table in the ballroom while Hailey walks to the front door to let them in.

Our next couple is a pair I swear could be brother and sister. Tom and Tara have matching auburn hair, blue eyes, both tall and thin with high cheekbones and full lips. They finish each other's sentences. It's so bizarre I'm speechless.

"Whatever you want, pookie-bear," Tom says.

"Teddy bear, I want what you want," Tara says.

"I love you," Tom says, rubbing his nose against hers.

"I love you more," Tara says.

"No, I love you more."

"I love you the mostest."

After twenty minutes, they haven't decided anything. I turn the page in the binder and point to a traditional white wedding cake with a topper. "How's this?"

"I was thinking—" Tara starts.

"Tiramisu," Tom and Tara finish in unison.

"Jinx!" Tara says. "You owe me a kiss."

Tom frames her face in his hands and gives her a tender kiss. My gut does a slow churn. They're so in love. Was I ever that in love? Dave never loved me. Not really. If he had, we'd be married. Instead he's with Sheila and her llamas.

When they finally come up for air, Hailey says brightly, "It's refreshing to meet such a happy couple. Would you like to host your wedding here or at a church? We can accommodate either."

"Here would be good," Tara says.

"Yes," Tom says. "As long as you can accommodate a priest and a rabbi."

"Absolutely," Hailey says. "We've had many interfaith ceremonies. Let me look at some dates for you."

"We want it on Christmas Day," Tom says. "That's the anniversary of our first date. We met at a friend's Christmas party."

"We're closed on Christmas," I say. "Right, Hailey?"

"We are. Might I suggest a warm-weather day?"

"I freckle in the sun," Tara says.

"Your freckles are beautiful," Tom says.

"Really? Did you see my neck recently?"

He nuzzles her neck, and she squeals.

I look away. Their happiness has nothing to do with me. This is business. I shouldn't feel bad that I never had that absolute adoration.

"How about Easter Sunday?" Tara asks. "I love chocolate bunnies. We can decorate the place with chocolate bunnies and hide Easter eggs."

Tom gives Tara a gentle smile. "My family might not be keen on the Easter symbolism, pookie bear. How about Purim?"

"What's Purim again?" Tara asks.

"How about we avoid holidays altogether?" I ask. "You could have a beautiful spring or summer wedding on a random Saturday."

I glance at Hailey. She doesn't look happy.

"Random?" Tom asks. "It's like you don't think the date signifies anything."

"It's supposed to be our special day," Tara says. "Meaningful to us." She turns to Hailey. "I thought you said this was a place where the clients' needs come first."

"It is!" Hailey exclaims.

"You sound bitter," Tom says to me. "Did your own wedding not go as planned?"

My face gets hot.

"She's single," Tara says. "Look at her finger."

"I can see why," he says under his breath.

She giggles.

I'm halfway between shame and fury. Shame wins out, nausea roiling in my stomach. I leap from my seat and dash to the bathroom.

I splash cold water on my face, and the nausea passes. Grabbing a paper towel, I dab my face dry and stare at myself in the mirror. I don't think I can do this job. It's too much to see the lovey-dovey couples, the squabbling over details. None of that matters. It's supposed to be about love.

A tear escapes. I let Hailey down again after all she's done for me. I can't afford to lose this job. First of all, I owe her for my own wedding. Second, no one's going to give me the flexibility Hailey promised so I can get my own life back together. And I sincerely want to help. She's a really nice person; her whole family is too. Not singling any one out in particular. Just saying. Good people.

I shift and rest my forehead against the cool wall, trying to think. Can I go back in there? Is Hailey going to fire me?

Maybe I'll just stay in this bathroom forever. I sink to the floor, bending my knees and wrapping my arms around them. I rest my head against my arm, exhausted by emotional turmoil.

I'm not sure how much time has passed when there's a knock at the door. I lift my head.

"Rowan?" Hailey says. "Can I come in?"

I stand and open the door. She gives me a sympathetic look, takes my hand, and pulls me out to the hallway.

"I'm sorry," I say.

She gives my arm a squeeze. "Nothing to be sorry about. It's too soon for you to meet with clients. *I'm* sorry I put you through that. I'm sure it's bringing back lots of unpleasant memories."

I nod, my eyes stinging.

She puts an arm around my shoulders and guides me to her office. "You'll be my back office support, okay? Let's get you started on the accounting software."

"Did Tara and Tom leave?"

"Yes, we finished. You were in the bathroom for a long time."

"I wasn't sure if I could face them again, and I was afraid you'd fire me."

She stops, putting her hands on my shoulders and meeting my eyes. "You had a bumpy first day, but I have complete confidence you can be a great help in many other areas."

"Thanks for a second chance."

She hugs me, and I relax, enveloped by her motherly care. "No problem at all."

I settle at my desk and log on to the accounting software, happily learning how to help in a way I'm good at.

Love's not in my future, but at least I can focus on work.

8

I get to Ludbury House bright and early the next day. Today I'll be the ultimate assistant.

"Good morning!" Hailey says with a sunny smile as she walks up the front path. "Looks like you're as much of an early bird as I am. I'm up at dawn and already got my workout in."

"Morning! Looking forward to whatever you need me to do." I debate throwing in another apology for my meltdown yesterday, but decide it's better not to remind her.

She does the security code on a keypad near the door to disable the alarm system, unlocks the door with a key, and walks in.

I follow her.

She opens the door to her office. "Today I'll have you catch up on entering all the invoices into the accounting system. Then we'll talk about marketing to keep business coming in. Sound good?"

"Absolutely."

She walks to her desk and boots up her laptop. She goes to Ally's old laptop, turns it on and logs on, clicking over to settings. She sets it up for a new password for me to enter.

"There. Now you can unlock the laptop with the password of your choosing. Just make sure to let me know what it is. Make it memorable."

I type it in as I speak. "Secondchance26."

"Are you twenty-six?"

"Yeah. Guess it's not that original."

"It's great. And I like the optimism. You're giving happiness a second chance. You'll be in top form in no time."

My eyebrows scrunch together. I hadn't meant happiness. I meant Hailey's giving me a second chance. Oh well, I don't want to continually remind her how badly I screwed up yesterday and need a second chance. I'll go with her more optimistic take.

She drops a bulging folder on my desk. "Here's the invoices and receipts. I print out everything. Open up the accounting software, and I'll show you how to enter them. I'm two weeks behind billing people. Some of these are already paid, but not entered in the system. Some of them are open."

Like my bill. I shudder to think how large it is. We paid a twenty-five percent deposit. I was in denial about costs when I planned everything. Of course, I hadn't thought my business would be starting from zero either.

I click to open the software. "I did the tutorial yesterday, so I'm familiar."

She smiles. "Great. I'll just show you the way we do it here, and then you'll be up and running."

I take careful notes as she shows me how to enter each piece of data. I can't screw up again.

"You understand?" she asks.

"Yes. You can count on me."

"I'm sure I can. I expect this to take you all morning. After lunch, I'll go over ongoing marketing. I like to get the word out around Christmas, New Year's, and Valentine's Day when a lot of couples get engaged."

"Of course. I know the ad world well."

She smiles and goes to her desk. "I have a lunch date with

a friend today. I asked Cooper to stop by with some takeout for you."

The hair on the back of my neck stands up. Matchmaker alert!

"Oh, that's not necessary."

"Did you bring lunch today?"

"No, but—"

"You have to eat." She puts on a phone headset and makes a call. "Hi, Hailey Campbell here from Love Junkies. How are you?"

I put my head down and do my work. I don't want to put Cooper out. He's probably working, and his mom *made* him help me out with lunch. I can just walk back to Mackenzie's house and make myself a sandwich. I bought peanut butter and jelly, which should last a long time. Note to self: bring sandwich to work every day.

It takes me two hours, but I get everything into the system. "I finished," I announce.

"Okay, I'll look it over, and then, once I give the okay, you can shred the paper trail."

"It would be more efficient to keep all the emailed invoices and receipts in a shared folder on the computer; then I can enter it from there. Electronic records are just as good and better for the environment."

"Look at you already improving the office and the environment. Guess I'm still old school with the paper trail. Okay, we'll try it your way going forward, but I'd like to keep the paper trail from old stuff."

I smile. See, I'm already proving myself. "Can I see your marketing materials?"

"Yup. There's some on your computer, some on mine, and in that file cabinet behind you."

I turn to a tall wooden file cabinet behind me and rifle through two drawers full of ads, photos, and documents. Whoa. "Do you use all this stuff?"

"We rotate. I like to keep the files so we can go through and pick out the season."

"But there's no labels by season."

"It's in the order of which type of ad I use the most. A relevancy system." She presses her headset. "Hello, Hailey Campbell, Love Junkies, how can I help you?"

I should be answering the phone for new clients, right? She must be constantly interrupted. On the other hand, I didn't do so well dealing directly with clients. I'll stick to being the best damn behind-the-scenes helper she could ever want.

Cooper

I walk into Ludbury House with a Cobb salad for Rowan as requested. Mom says she's working out great, and she's a wonderful woman. I think that last part was for my benefit. As always, Mom's hoping for a love connection. I'm thinking more casual.

I walk up the steps to Ludbury House and press the bell. I can see through the glass panel next to the door the moment Rowan appears in the foyer. She smooths her brown hair back and adjusts her skirt like she's nervous. I wonder if she's thought about that kiss as much as I have.

She opens the door. "Hi! You really didn't have to take time off work to bring me lunch."

I hand her the bag. "You're welcome."

"Sorry! Thank you! I just feel bad your mom made you bring me lunch."

"Mom hasn't made me do anything in a long time."

"Right. Ha! Of course. You're a grown man."

"She told me your order, and I volunteered to bring it. There's a sandwich in there for me too. Mind if I join you?"

She backs up a step. "Sure. It's just me here."

"I know. Mom's having lunch with my aunt Madison. They're like oil and water but best friends."

"Cool."

I step inside and shut the door behind me. She heads

toward the kitchen. She's dressed nice in a V-neck sweater and skirt that hugs her curves. So sexy.

We get to the kitchen, and she unpacks the bag. I go for glasses of water, napkins, and a fork for her.

Once we're settled at the table, she opens her takeout container. "Oh, Cobb salad. That's nice."

I take out my roast beef sandwich. "Isn't that what you ordered?"

"Actually, your mom ordered it for me. I thought maybe she was matchmaking."

"She's just thoughtful." *Definitely matchmaking.* I'm going to have to have a talk with her. I don't want Mom getting her hopes up that Rowan's the One. Mom's big on meeting the One. If I knew Rowan was going to stick around, if Rowan hadn't just been dumped at her wedding, and if I hadn't been burned by Brianna before, then maybe I could be open to something more. But all of those things did happen, so here we are. Friends who kissed once.

We dig into lunch.

She gives me a small smile. "It's good."

"Glad to hear it."

"Can I have some of your chips?"

I push my container closer to her. "So you're not the health nut Mom is."

"I want to eat healthy, but it's just so boring."

I laugh. "So how's it working out here?"

"Oh, Cooper, I'm so embarrassed."

"Why?"

Then she tells me how she messed up both wedding consultations yesterday and feared she was going to be fired after just one day.

"First days can be rough," I say. "You're just getting the hang of things."

"Your mom stuck me in the office permanently for behind-the-scenes work."

I shake my head, smiling. "I'm sure she'll let you out for good behavior."

"I guess I wasn't ready to relive the whole bridal experience."

"Can't blame you."

She goes back to her lunch, so I do the same. After a while she says, "I owe your mom for my wedding bill. It's thousands, so I guess I'll be here a while working off my debt."

"You make it sound like you're stuck. I'm sure you can work out a payment plan. She wants you to get back on your feet. That's why she offered a flexible job."

"Did you tell her all the details?"

"Yeah. Before Sunday dinner."

She frowns. "How many other people did you tell?"

I hold up a palm. "Just her and only because I knew she could help you. She's so well connected in town and the surrounding area. I didn't know she'd offer to let you live with her and offer you a job. That was all her."

"I don't want to broadcast the fact that I was screwed over by the man I was about to marry."

"She won't say a word, and neither will I. You can count on Mackenzie and Harper being discreet too. Well, Harper might leap to your defense, but if you ask her not to say anything, she won't."

"Wow. I guess it's not exactly a secret anymore."

"A select few are in the know. Do you miss the city?"

"Yeah, I do. I'm a fish out of water here. Seems like everyone knows everyone. The pace is slower." She smiles. "Still getting used to how friendly everyone is. Why are you so easy to talk to?"

I grin. "Guess it's all that listening I do at the bar. Boy, can people talk with a few drinks in them."

"I'm sure."

"And I want to listen to you."

Her hand goes to her neck. "I don't want you to get the wrong idea. The other day, that thing that happened—"

"You kissed me."

"No, you kissed me."

"That's not how I remember it."

Her brows scrunch together. "I'm not sure how that happened, but it was a mistake."

"You kissed me by accident?"

"No, the other way. Whatever. It was a mistake."

I meet her eyes. "It's hard to deny there's something between us. Chemistry, connection."

She waves that away. "It doesn't matter what's here or not here. Maybe I'm just feeling desperately alone at the moment, but it's not anything I want to follow up on. Cooper, I'm a wreck on the inside."

"I'll be gentle."

"You'll be…that's not…" She crosses her arms. "We're friends. End of story."

"Okay." Never argue with a woman who's digging her heels in. I've seen it firsthand with past relationships. Not to mention every female family member. Lotta strong opinionated women in my family.

She uncrosses her arms. "Okay?"

"Yup. Friends." I finish my sandwich in a few bites. "Want more chips?"

"No, thank you."

I finish the chips and gather the trash, taking it to the garbage can in the corner. I can feel her eyes on me. She doesn't know what to make of my casual acceptance of the friends situation.

I return to the table and finish my water. "Nice to see you, Rowan. Hope your second day goes better than your first."

She stands. "Oh, uh, thank you."

"Bye."

I head out. I make it to the foyer before I hear footsteps behind me.

"Wait!" she calls.

I turn, fighting back a smile. *She wants me.* "Yeah?"

"Thank you for lunch. It was nice not to eat alone."

"Anytime. I'm usually working across the street, but I'm off Wednesdays and Sundays. That's my weekend." I hold my palm out. "Give me your phone, and I'll put my number in."

She strides to the office to get it. I follow her, nearly colliding with her in the doorway as she rushes back. She slaps a hand on my chest and quickly drops it. Her eyes meet mine, and she licks her lips. My pulse spikes. *I want her too. So bad.*

"Sorry to slap your chest," she says, handing me her phone. "Didn't expect to walk into you like that."

I enter my number. "No problem. You know the city's only an hour and fifteen minutes away by train. It's not lost to you forever."

She laughs. "Yeah. Sometimes I feel like I dropped into another world. You're right."

I give her phone back, and our fingers brush against each other. Warmth shoots up my arm. Definitely some chemistry here.

She pushes her hair behind her ear. "Thanks."

"When I was a kid, my parents took us into the city to visit the American Museum of Natural History. The planetarium really stuck with me."

She leans close in her excitement. "The Hayden Planetarium is awesome."

"I'd love to see it again one day." I take a step back. "Welp, I'd better get back to work."

She waves. "Sure. Bye."

"Bye." I push open the door.

"We could go places as friends," she blurts. "Like the Hayden Planetarium since you like it so much."

I turn in the doorway. "It's a date."

She cocks her head. "Ha-ha. I'd better get back to work." She rushes to the office.

See what I did there? *Smooth move, Cooper.*

9

———

Rowan

By Friday, I'm in a groove at Love Junkies, launching Hailey's winter marketing campaign, as well as digging into online marketing to get some buzz. I even started social media accounts for Love Junkies. All they had was a business page on one of the social media channels that they never updated. I can't believe I'm the voice behind a place called Love Junkies considering I'm the farthest thing from a love junkie. I'm now staunchly anti-love like Mackenzie. I was never much of a romantic, and Dave killed whatever shred of romanticism was left in me.

Hailey stops by at the end of the day after finishing three back-to-back consultations. "How's it going in here?"

"Great. I set up some low-cost online ads for you like we talked about. It might be good to update a blog on your website with relevant keywords. It'll bring you up in searches more. Maybe even get some free publicity with your articles."

She points at me. "Sounds like a great job for my assistant."

"But I don't know anything about bridal articles."

"I'll give you some ideas, and you run with it. I trust you."

"I really appreciate that trust, but—"

"Did you know that last couple mentioned they followed

us on all the social media platforms? I checked, and we already have hundreds of followers. How did you do that?"

"I've been posting pictures you have in the marketing campaign folders with fun captions. I also found popular hashtags and glommed on to that."

She parks a hand on her hip. "Aren't you a wonder? I'm so glad I hired you." She goes to her drawer and pulls out an envelope. "Here's your first paycheck for the week."

I walk over and take it. "Thank you, but I thought I was going to work off my debt."

She gives me a small smile. "About that. I'm going to take off my personal fee from your wedding. We'll work out a payment plan, okay? You go ahead and crunch the numbers and pay me back as much as you can afford. I want you to start rebuilding your savings. I know you'll need it to move on."

"Right." Move on. Just like I've been planning this whole time. Back to the city and my old life.

But do I want that? I'm actually more comfortable and relaxed in Clover Park than I've been in a long, long time. It's a beautiful town with wonderful people. Not a lot to do, but I'm really connecting with people in a way that I wasn't in the city. We were all too busy.

I haven't even tried to find new business for my solo ad agency. I just need a breather before I make the hard decisions, like whether to give up the career I've spent years building and find something else that works for me. Clover Park is my breather while I wait for my condo deposit and for my case to be heard in small claims court. I suppose I could get started on researching new possible careers and see if anything appeals.

Hailey puts on a cardigan and gets her purse from her desk drawer. "I'll see you tomorrow morning for setup for the Rothchild-Smith wedding. You should be done by noon."

"Yup." I get my purse and light jacket and follow her out. She locks up and sets the security alarm.

"Any plans this weekend?" she asks.

"Other than trying to figure out what I want to do with my life? No."

"Maybe Mackenzie and Harper will have something fun you can do together. And you're welcome for Sunday family dinner."

"I'll be there for dinner, thanks," I say.

She gives my arm a squeeze. "Have a good night." She heads to the back parking lot for her car.

I stand on the porch for a moment, enjoying the crisp fall breeze and the pops of color in the trees. One day I'll look back on this and see it as a gift. A fresh start to a life of my choosing.

I walk across the street, my eye catching on the Happy Endings bar sign. Cooper's probably working tonight. No. I'm not going to stop by. I need to go home and figure stuff out. I peek at my paycheck. After taxes, it's…a start. I'll work out a payment plan and share it with Hailey on Monday.

I head down the block to Mackenzie and Harper's house. My phone chimes with a text.

Cooper: *Hayden Planetarium on Sunday? A friend told me it's awesome.*

I find myself smiling. I'm the friend. I text back: *Okay, but I have to be back in time for Sunday family dinner.*

Cooper: *Or we could get a bite to eat in the city.*

So casual. It really does sound like this can work as friends. On the other hand, I already accepted Hailey's invitation.

Me: *We'll go early and get back in time for dinner.*

Cooper: *How early?*

Me: *I'll get back to you on that.*

Cooper: *Stop by for a drink tonight. On the house.*

I shake my head. One drink can lead to so much more. Not going there.

I text back: *Thanks, but I have a lot of stuff to figure out.*

A few minutes later, I let myself into the house. It's so quiet. Felix appears and winds around my leg. I reach down to pet him, and he stands on his hind legs to stretch against my leg, his head arching for more.

"Hello?" I call.

I hang my jacket and purse on a hook by the door and leave my shoes by the mat there. I have to say Mackenzie makes the place feel like home. She even added me to the chore rotation. My job is to empty the dishwasher and take out the trash on Sunday. Next week I get to do meal planning and prep for three meals. It's all on a spreadsheet she emails to me and Harper on Monday night. Apparently, she was an accounting major, so she's very comfortable with spreadsheets. Harper says Mackenzie basically runs the security tech firm she's partners in with Owen and Nathan.

I walk upstairs and poke my head into Mackenzie's room. She's not there. Outfits are strewn all over the bed and a chair. Does she have a date?

I step out into the hall. Sounds like the shower's running in our shared hall bathroom.

Harper's door is shut. She's probably working on a graphic design project. Whenever she works from home, she likes to sleep in and work later hours. I won't disturb her.

I head downstairs and nearly trip over Felix waiting for me on the first step down. I scoop him up. "I won't be around to pet you if you kill me on the stairs."

He purrs and rubs against my chest. I relax holding this warm bundle of fur. It's like coming home to a warm hug. I can use a hug.

Once in the kitchen, I help myself to the last little bit of leftover lasagna and pop it in the microwave. It's Harper's week to cook, and she likes to make two giant dishes for us to eat as leftovers the entire week. Mackenzie calls this lazy, and Harper calls it efficient. I'm just happy to have a home-cooked meal.

I'm nearly done with dinner when Mackenzie walks in, adjusting a dangling earring. Her hair falls in soft waves, subtle makeup. She's wearing a cute light blue pants suit with heels.

"Hey," she says. "How was work at love heaven?"

"Good. Your mom's great to work for. We worked out a behind-the-scenes position for me since I'm anti-love at the moment."

She gives me a fist bump. "Solidarity, sister. Mom said she invited you to Sunday family dinner. Please don't feel obligated to go because your boss invited you. Not that I don't want you there. I'm just saying that's a lot of Hailey time. After working all week with her and half of Saturday when there's a wedding, you might need a break."

"Not at all. I could hang with her all day every day."

She crinkles her nose. "I guess she's easier to take when she's not prying into your love life." She gets a drink of water and leans against the counter.

I rinse my plate and put it in the dishwasher. "Date tonight?"

"Kinda. I don't know what it is."

"What's the plan?"

"Meeting for drinks at a nice restaurant with a bar. Not Happy Endings. Don't need Dad and Cooper spying on me. Harper's going to call after fifteen minutes, and if I'm having a wretched time, I'm claiming a family emergency and leaving. If not, we'll see how it goes."

"Smart. How'd you meet?"

"He was my assigned groomsman at a friend's wedding. Drop-dead gorgeous, but I'm afraid a little boring. He's a lawyer at his father's law firm."

"Maybe he won't be so boring once you get to know him."

"I just need to see if drop-dead gorgeous means chemistry. I had a little too much of the open bar at the wedding to tell if it was true chemistry or drink-fueled lust. Have I mentioned how much I hate the forced coupledom at weddings?" She adjusts her pants suit and unbuttons the top button. "How do I look?"

"Sexy?"

She laughs. "Not sure why that came out as a question,

but I'll take it. Harper's working late with a midnight deadline. TV remote's all yours tonight. Enjoy the power!"

Felix walks in with a shaky tail as he rubs against a chair leg.

"There's my little meow-meow," Mackenzie coos.

He goes to her, and she picks him up, cuddling her face against his. She makes kissy noises at him and sets him down.

"Bye!"

"Bye! Hope you have fun."

She leaves, and I turn to Felix. "We can figure out my life or binge-watch something more dramatic than my life."

He stares at me with a hint of skepticism.

"Well, we can hope there's something more dramatic. Geez."

I lead the way to the living room and nearly trip as he dashes ahead of me and then circles back between my legs. "Again, I can't pet you if you kill me."

There's a second TV in the living room in case Harper hogs the TV in the front room to play her favorite fantasy video game. After surfing channels for a while, I start feeling restless. I don't want to sit home alone on a Friday night. My life's not over because Dave's not in it.

"I'm going out," I announce to Felix as I shift him off me and get up.

He gives me a perturbed look for ruining his Friday night.

"I'll be back."

He's already moved on, leaping to the warm spot on the sofa where I just was.

I make the short walk to Happy Endings. It's okay to hang with Cooper as friends. I need a friend, and he's been a good one to me.

But when I get there, Cooper's leaning across the bar in deep conversation with a brunette woman in a tight skirt.

I avoid them and go to the far corner of the bar to observe. She's young, beautiful, and delighted by whatever he's saying. He's smiling, looking charming as ever. I'm *not* jealous. Why would I be jealous of a friend?

He catches my eye, and I quickly look away. I don't want him to think I'm spying.

A moment later, he's in front of me. "I was hoping you'd stop by tonight. What can I get you?"

The beautiful brunette joins us, leaning across the bar to kiss his cheek. "Always a happy ending with you. Don't forget about my showing!"

He inclines his head. "I'll be there. Good to see you again, Rachel."

Rachel flashes a smile and heads out.

"She seems nice," I say.

"What can I get you, beautiful?"

"Don't do that."

"Do what?"

"Call me beautiful. We're friends."

"Right."

He looks at me expectantly.

"I'll take whatever's your cheapest white wine, please," I say.

"It's on the house," he says. "Let me get you the good stuff. We have a fantastic chardonnay from California."

"I got paid today, so I've got it." My voice sounds snippier than I'd like. I just find it odd that there's a parade of grateful beautiful women who seek him out. First there was Gina on the day we met. She invited him back to her place, and now this woman Rachel wants him to go to some kind of showing.

He retrieves a bottle of chardonnay that I assume is the cheap stuff because I was very clear I'm paying my own way here. After he hands me a glass of wine, he says, "What's wrong? You're frowning more than usual. Bad news from your ex?"

"No. Things are okay. I have a date for small claims court in four weeks. Hopefully I'll win and get some compensation for what he stole."

"Isn't your dad a lawyer? He could probably represent you and make it a slam dunk."

I stare at him. "You remember that from the day we met?"

"I remember everything you tell me."

"Do you remember everything Gina and Rachel tell you too?"

He puts his palms up. "Whoa. Green-eyed monster came out to play."

I take a gulp of wine. It's wonderful. I think he tricked me with the good stuff. "Why would I be jealous? We're just friends. Obviously, I'm not looking for a relationship. In fact, the idea makes me want to puke."

"When did you meet Gina?"

"The day of my wedding. I came in here, and she invited you to her place."

He thinks for a moment. "Oh, yeah. She wanted to show me her apartment. I found an affordable place for her in a nice neighborhood in Eastman next door."

"Not my concern."

"I'm an open book. You can ask me anything."

I press my lips together, not wanting to ask about Rachel. It's really not like me to care who a guy I like as a friend talks to. I blame my ex. Once you've been betrayed, it's hard to trust any man.

I take a sip of wine. "I saw Dave's most recent social media post of him, Sheila, and a llama. They look very happy together."

"*Blech.*"

"I immediately blocked all his accounts. It's enough to know he's moved on. I don't need to see it too."

He leans an elbow against the bar, close enough I can breathe in his woodsy scent. He's so sexy. Anyone would think so. "Smart."

What if I posted a picture of me and Cooper online? #Revengepost

"You have a look of intrigue," he says. "Plotting something?"

I decide not to go there. That might give Cooper the wrong idea. "Just thinking. I guess having a near-death experience made Dave reevaluate his life. In some way, I went through similar with the death of my relationship and the future I thought I'd have. I'm reevaluating too."

He holds up a finger to me and goes to pour beers for a couple of guys at the other end of the bar. He returns to me.

"Mackenzie's on a date tonight with a lawyer," I say.

"Good for her."

"She fears he's too boring."

"Well, I'm sure she'll find out soon enough." He leans across the bar, his eyes warm, his voice smooth as silk. "I'm glad you're reevaluating your life. Gives me a chance to get to know you better."

"Cooper!" a feminine voice exclaims. I turn to see a stunning woman with sleek black hair approach. She looks like she just stepped off the runway.

"Hey, Vickie," he says warmly. "You're back. How was Milan?"

She leans across the bar and air-kisses him on both cheeks. "Fantastic. I owe my life to you."

"Not at all. You had a dream. Mom needed a model."

"How is your mom? I just love her to pieces."

"Doing well. Actually, Rowan here is working with her over at Love Junkies."

Vickie smiles at me. "Don't you just love all the stunning wedding gowns going through that place?"

"Mmm-hmm," I say noncommittally.

"Sparkling water?" he asks her.

"You know me so well. Actually, I can't stay. I'm meeting some friends in the city for dinner, but this was my first stop after the airport. I was at that little one for private planes. A group jet share. I'm not that big a name. Yet."

I stare at her. No one looks that good stepping off a long international flight. Who is she kidding?

"I'm flattered I was your first stop," Cooper says.

She turns to me. "What's Cooper helping you out with? The man is a miracle worker. Just bring him a problem and he helps you in a way you never dreamed possible."

I'm not rehashing my life with a stranger, especially a glamorous woman living the high life.

"We're friends," I say. "I'm new in town."

Her brows scrunch in confusion. "Friends? Cooper doesn't do women friends." She laughs. "Maybe he does do them."

"Get outta here," Cooper says. "No sparkling water for you."

She wiggles her fingers at him. "Ciao."

He smiles. "Ciao."

She leaves, and he watches her go, still smiling. My gut churns. I toss back my wine and throw a bunch of dollar bills on the bar top. I have no idea how much that wine cost, but hopefully that covers it.

He glances at the pile of money. "I told you it's on the house."

"I'm not your charity case. I can see that's what you're running here with all these women."

"What women?"

"Puh-lease. Two women appeared in the last fifteen minutes falling all over themselves for whatever you did for them. I appreciate your kindness, but I don't want to be one of a long line of women you rescue or whatever."

"Are you done?"

I press my lips in a flat line. "Yes."

"I didn't rescue anyone. I just lend an ear and make a connection for people if I have one. I'm second generation here with a large extended family, all local. With all the businesses of friends and family, I'm in a position to be helpful. I'm better than the internet because I can vouch for them."

"It's so annoying how good you are."

"You like the bad boys?"

I lift my chin. "I'm in love with my roommate's cat. That's the only bad boy or any male I want close to me for the fore-seeable future."

"Fair enough."

I frown, studying the bar top. Another glass of that delicious wine magically appears. My wad of crumpled bills lies on the bar untouched. I shove them in a tip jar nearby.

I sip it, relaxing a little. Cooper goes to take care of other customers. I guess I was hogging his attention on a Friday night. I need to chill. He's warm and friendly with everyone —man, woman, young, old.

I finish my wine, slightly buzzed, and slide off the barstool.

"Let me walk you home," Cooper says, signaling for a waiter to take over.

"I'm okay."

He joins me, standing so close I'm tempted to lean in to him and breathe deep. Why is he so close? I step back, and he's smiling at me. Was I the one who moved into his personal space?

"I'm on break," he says. "I like to take a walk on break and get some quiet and fresh air."

"Oh. Okay."

We walk to the front door, and he holds it open for me.

"I bought tickets ahead of time for the planetarium show on Sunday," he says. "Wanted to make sure we had our choice of shows before it sold out."

"Thank you. That was thoughtful."

We start walking. His fingers brush against mine, sending tingles up my arm. "You're welcome. I thought we could head into the city early, grab some lunch, and walk around before we get to the planetarium."

"Sounds fun."

"I thought so." He looks to the sky, where the stars seem brighter here. "I admit I know nothing about the constellations."

"There's the Big Dipper. That one's always easy to find."

He stares at it while walking and stumbles on a sidewalk crack. I grab his arm to steady him. Damn, that is one muscled arm.

He smiles. "Thanks for the quick save."

"Work out much?"

He laughs. "I stay fit."

"Your bicep's like a rock."

"Thank you."

He flexes comically. I'm both turned on and entertained. I've never met a guy like him before. Gorgeous but not arrogant about it, warm and caring for everyone he meets.

"Ridiculous," I say.

"Let's see yours."

I push up my sleeve and flex my bicep, hoping that something's showing. There's a slight curve.

He nods. "Impressive. Almost the size of a lime."

"Squeeze me on your margarita." I laugh. "I can't believe I said that. I think that wine went to my head. I had a small dinner."

"That's not good."

"I had a late lunch, and then I was caught up in work. Don't worry, I'll grab something at home."

"I'm not worried."

We get to my house, and he stops. "See you Sunday. We can catch the ten a.m. train. I'll pick you up."

He's close again, kissing close. Is that me or him moving in? "Are you trying to kiss me again?"

His lips curve up, his eyes searching mine. "Do you want me to kiss you again?"

Yes. I try to be logical for his sake. "Friends don't kiss."

"What about friends with benefits?"

My lips part. I hadn't considered that option.

He backs up a step. "See ya soon, beautiful."

I stare at him, still caught up in the tantalizing idea of a friends-with-benefits situation. I've never had one of those. "Bye, gorgeous."

He grins and swaggers into the night.

Ooh, boy, I'm playing with fire.

10

———

Cooper

I ring the bell at Mackenzie and Harper's place to pick up Rowan on Sunday, and Mackenzie answers the door. She's an early bird like Mom.

"Hi." She steps outside and shuts the door behind her. "Seems like you're spending a lot of time with Rowan."

"Problem?"

"Coop, she's two weeks out from her wedding. You don't want to be her rebound."

"Let me worry about that."

"This is just like Brianna. You rescue her, get involved, and then you're the one who gets hurt." She squeezes my shoulder. "I just don't want you to get your heart broken again."

I shake my head. "It's casual. No big."

She gives me a skeptical look, turns, and opens the door for me.

I step inside just as Rowan rushes in from the kitchen, her eyes bright. She's wearing a snug pink V-neck sweater and jeans. My pulse thrums in my veins. "Hi! Just finished taking care of Felix. Ready for a Sunday funday."

I laugh. "Sounds good to me." I turn to Mackenzie. "See you at Sunday family dinner tonight."

She waves and smiles, acting casual for Rowan's benefit. "Have fun, you two. But not too much fun."

We head for my car for the short drive to the train station. Easier than dealing with parking in the city. I open the passenger-side door for her.

"Wow, is this more of those gentleman manners you grew up with?" she asks, standing close to me. She smells like citrus and something uniquely her.

"Get used to it. Ingrained in me from birth. You should've seen me opening doors for Mackenzie when I was in kindergarten. She would shut them and open them herself."

"Ha! I could see that." She gets in, and I shut the door behind her.

I jog to the other side, eager to get on with the day. As soon as I get in the car, she says, "This isn't a date, just so we're clear."

"I didn't think it was. Just two friends enjoying each other's company." I pull onto the street. "I was joking around before when I said it's a date."

"You were?"

"Yeah, I joke a lot."

"Okay."

I can feel her studying me as I drive. "Really."

"Okay, awesome. I know a ton of great places for lunch by the museum. And we have to stop by my favorite candy shop. It's expensive, but you can buy individual pieces."

"Cool."

She launches enthusiastically into a list of places for lunch. I smile to myself. She sounds happy. I don't know if it's me or a trip to the city, but it's great to hear. She's not like Brianna. She's strong and resilient, someone I don't need to rescue. I can just enjoy being with her.

Mackenzie's voice rings in my head: *rebound, rebound, rebound.* I push that away. It's just a fun day in the city.

∼

Rowan

After a delicious lunch at an Italian restaurant, Cooper and I check in at the American Museum of Natural History with the tickets he bought in advance. There's a large crowd here as usual on the weekend.

"I'll reimburse you," I say, reaching for my purse. "You got lunch."

"Don't worry about it."

"I have a paycheck now."

He looks around. "Which way to the planetarium?" He points the way and then reaches for my hand. "Don't want to lose you in the crowd."

I gulp. His larger hand envelops mine in warmth. Do friends hold hands? I don't say a word because I'm enjoying it too much. It's both exciting and calming at the same time.

He leads the way to the planetarium.

When we get there, I pull my hand away, relieved to not be touching him. He's just too tempting. I can't get involved so soon after my breakup. I'm not sure I want to risk even a friends-with-benefits situation with Cooper. What if I get attached?

"Best view is in the back row," I say.

We settle into the back row. It's dim in here with constella-tions on the ceiling. People are still filing in.

I pull out my phone. "Let's take a selfie."

He leans close and smiles. God, he's gorgeous. I snap the picture and post it to my social with the caption: "This guy makes me see stars. Hayden Planetarium fun!" I tag the museum in it too. I'm sure it'll help them to have people post about how cool it is here.

I show him the picture.

"I guess I did make you see stars since this was my idea."

"Yeah. Thought it would help out the museum. They like when you tag them. I like to fit in a visit a few times a year. After this, we should check out Lucy. She's a three-million-year-old full skeleton of an early human."

"I'll follow your lead." His voice sounds husky. A shiver runs down my spine.

The show starts, and I lean back in my seat to take in the best view of the cosmos you can get. I find myself glancing at Cooper regularly to see if he's enjoying it too. He meets my gaze with a smile that makes my heart beat faster.

I should stop looking at him so much.

After the show ends, we stand. He takes my hand and leads the way through the crowd. It feels so natural to hold hands with him. Is that weird?

Once we're clear of the crowd, I point toward the elevators. "We need to get to the first floor for the Human Origins exhibit."

We get in line at the elevator and cram in with everyone else. I'm shoulder to shoulder with Cooper, our arms pressed against each other.

"Good thing I'm not claustrophobic," Cooper says.

I laugh and so do several other people.

We step out and cross through the main gallery.

"Rowan!" a familiar male voice calls.

I freeze and instinctively take Cooper's hand. He sends me a questioning look.

"It's Dave," I whisper.

Dave jogs up to us. "Are you with him now?"

"How did you know I was here?"

"I saw your post. So this guy makes you see stars?"

Cooper's arm drapes across my shoulders. "That's right. Your loss is my gain."

"Excuse us, we have a lot to talk about," Dave says.

"Whatever you have to say, you can say in front of Cooper," I say.

Dave glares at Cooper, who stands his ground.

Dave lowers his voice. "I miss you. Sheila won't take care of me the way you do. I miss the way you always made sure I had a hot meal, did the laundry, and kept the place nice. It felt like home."

"Hire a cleaning service," I say. "I'm tired of taking care of people. I want to be with someone who's a true partner. Someone who stands on his own two feet."

His face falls. "You did it because you loved me. I'm not sure Sheila loves me. I think she used me to get the llama farm."

I take a deep breath. I almost feel bad for him. Almost. "I've moved on."

Cooper kisses my temple like we're a couple. I flush with heat. I did want a revenge picture for Dave. I just hadn't thought an innocent planetarium photo would bring him out of the woodwork.

Dave's voice turns pleading. "I know I did a shitty thing bringing our clients to my cousin's firm. You can work there too. No one does the social media thing like you, and all that digital strategy and marketing stuff too. That was all you."

I sigh. "Go home, Dave."

"But—"

"You heard her," Cooper growls. "Get out of here before I drag you out by the collar."

Dave pulls at his collar, sends me a last pleading look, and leaves.

We start walking again.

"So that's the guy who blew up your life," Cooper says. "What did you see in him?"

"He used to be charming and super supportive. Probably because I took care of his life, both personal and professional. Honestly, he changed after nearly drowning in a kayaking accident a month before our wedding. I guess facing death made him reevaluate his life."

"And make a bunch of stupid decisions."

"Yeah, I think the wedding put extra pressure on his fragile state. I guess I didn't realize how far gone he was until he left. Maybe I didn't want to see it."

Cooper stops and takes both my hands in his. "If he apologized and made everything right, would you take him back?"

"No, because *I* don't make stupid decisions."

He kisses my forehead, which somehow feels intimate.

"Smart and beautiful." Our gazes collide, sparks firing between us. The crowd fades into the background. It's just us connecting on some primal level. I've never wanted someone so much in my life. It was never this spellbinding with Dave.

An announcement goes out over the loudspeakers, breaking the spell.

I shift away. "Well."

"Yeah."

We walk toward the Human Origins exhibit, a new tension between us. He doesn't hold my hand. Somehow that only makes me want him more. How do I resist an irresistible man?

Cooper

Dave's whiny voice rings in my head. *Oh, please take care of me, Rowan.* Loser. I don't believe Dave changed after a near-death experience. He was always a weasel, but Rowan didn't see it until he showed his true colors.

I follow Rowan to the next exhibit. We're on a whirlwind tour of all her favorites. We have to catch the four-ten train back to make it in time for Sunday family dinner. I told her it was no big deal to miss, but she insisted. She really likes my family. The feeling's mutual. Dad even said she seemed all right, which is high praise from him.

It's cool the way she fits in my life. That's temporary, I know. She'll be getting her condo deposit back in a couple of weeks, and then she'll head right back here to snatch up an apartment.

I could visit her. What am I doing? Mackenzie's right. This is a classic rebound situation. I need to keep my distance.

"We can't miss the amethyst crystals," she says, practically running toward the hall with the big blue whale. "We'll go there after the whale."

"Slow down."

She looks at me over her shoulder. "We only have half an

hour left before we have to go to the train station." *Bam!* She collides with a large man and stumbles backward, losing her footing.

I lunge and catch her just in time. People applaud. The large man continues on his way.

She turns in my arms. "Thank you," she says softly. "You always seem to catch me when I fall."

My heart kicks up. "Just lucky, I guess."

I pull away first.

She takes my hand and leads the way. She initiated holding hands this time. That means she's comfortable with me.

My heart kicks harder. She wants me. I want her. This is a slippery slope, but I can't ignore this thing between us. As long as we spell out the rules before getting involved, no one will get hurt.

On the train ride home, Rowan holds my hand and falls asleep with her head on my shoulder.

In the car, she looks at me while I drive.

And when I park in front of my parents' house for Sunday family dinner, she says, "Would you like to be my friend with benefits?"

My lust shoots through the roof.

11

I've been thinking about the friends-with-benefits thing ever since Cooper first took my hand. Okay, before that, when we kissed. There's just something about him that makes me want to kiss him all over his gorgeous body and fuck like rabbits. I'm not ready for love, but I can't resist giving in to this attraction after today. He stood up for me in front of Dave. That means a lot.

He stares at me. "You ask me this in front of my parents' house? What're you doing to me?"

I glance down at the bulge in his jeans. "Oh, sorry. Forget I said that. We'll talk later."

"I can't forget you said that. It's out there like a big flashing Go sign."

"So you're into it?"

"Yeah, I'm into it."

I lean close to kiss him, and he pulls away. "What's wrong?"

"I need a walk around the block before walking into my parents' house. Stay there and don't do anything sexy."

I slowly lick my lips.

He groans, leans in for a quick kiss, and pulls away. "I'll see you when I'm presentable."

I smile and wiggle my fingers at him. This is going better than I thought. Maybe we should skip dinner and go straight to his place.

Nah, better not. We said we'd be here. I don't want his parents to conclude we're not there because we're fucking like rabbits. That's private.

Of course, it could give them the wrong idea if we show up together. Maybe I should go in. No, Mackenzie knows we went into the city together. She might slip and ask us about our day. I'll just say he gave me a ride.

That's the hope for later too. Ha-ha.

I wait on the sidewalk. Mackenzie pulls up with Finn. I wave. They get out of the car and join me.

"Look who I found sitting on the curb," Mackenzie says.

"Hey, Rowan," Finn says. He looks around. "Is Cooper inside already? I see his car."

"He took a walk."

"Why?" Mackenzie asks.

"Guess he needed to stretch his legs or something," I say.

"Did you two have a fight?" Mackenzie asks.

"Oh, no. Nothing like that. Go ahead in. He'll be back soon."

Mackenzie raises her brows at me. Somehow I think she knows there's something going on between us. Something more than friendship.

I shrug innocently.

"All right, we'll see you in there," Mackenzie says.

I look around for Cooper. He must've taken a longer walk than I thought he would. I figured he'd do once around the block.

Finally, he appears, a little out of breath.

"Are you okay?" I ask.

"Just sprinted to my house and back, thinking about moldy bread."

"Interesting. Moldy bread is a turnoff."

He does a double take and then laughs. "Come on, you."

I take my place at the table next to Cooper at his invitation. I'm not sure how I'm going to make it through this meal without spontaneously combusting. I can't help but imagine what we can do to each other after this. I feel like a horny teenager again, except I never did anything about it back then. Now's my chance.

Here comes the sexy part!

Not yet. Soon.

"How was the planetarium?" Mackenzie asks me and Cooper.

Hailey's eyes light up. "Oh, you two went together?"

"It was good," I say casually.

"How was your date with the lawyer?" Cooper asks Mackenzie.

"A lawyer?" Hailey exclaims. "Tell me everything."

Mackenzie presses her lips together. Cooper just turned Hailey's attention to her daughter's love life instead of his. Cooper and I exchange a secret triumphant look. He's good.

Mackenzie looks to her dad, then back to her mom. "At first I thought he was boring, but then I realized he's like Dad. Sort of unexciting but not completely boring."

"I'm not boring or unexciting!" Josh protests.

"Wonderful!" Hailey says. "Your dad is a great guy. I've been hoping you'd meet a wonderful man like him."

Mackenzie tilts her head thoughtfully. "He's not exactly like Dad. He's drop-dead gorgeous for one."

"I'm gorgeous," Josh says.

Hailey squeezes his arm. "Yes, you are, honey."

Mackenzie continues, "Honestly, I felt comfortable because he was a calm, grounded person."

"Dad's my rock," Hailey says. "This is great news! Do you have a picture?"

"No. I'm not sure if I'm going to see him again."

Josh huffs. "I am not a rock. Rocks are boring. I've led an exciting life. I used to jump out of airplanes in the Army."

Cooper sends me a conspiratorial look that says, isn't my family nutty? I grin.

Mackenzie sighs. "We know, Dad. You were a paratrooper."

He slaps his hand on the table. "I could jump out of an airplane right now. I've still got it."

Hailey smiles at him. "Nobody said you didn't, my warrior beast."

He huffs. "Lawyers are boring."

"What kind of lawyer is he?" Hailey asks Mackenzie.

"I didn't ask," Mackenzie says. "He's into walks in nature and never drinks or smokes."

"He sounds like someone coached him," Cooper says. "Like a dating profile. How do you know he's legit?"

Mackenzie ignores Cooper. "Anyway, he wants to take it slow to get to know me."

"That's good," Hailey says.

Mackenzie turns to me for understanding. "He wouldn't even kiss me good night for an experiment in chemistry. I think I'll leave him to a more patient woman. I need someone more fun. Not so much like Dad."

I nod sympathetically.

Josh pounds his chest. "I'm fun! Have you seen me on the dance floor?"

"Dad, you only slow dance," Mackenzie says.

"But I'm good at it. And nobody does a wild Saturday night like I do."

Hailey holds back a smile.

"Right, warrior princess?" Josh's voice holds a note of concern.

"Right."

Cooper gives his dad a deadpan look. "Yeah, I don't think we need the sexy play-by-play of your Saturday nights in with Mom."

Mackenzie, Cooper, and Finn laugh uproariously. Josh gives them a quelling look. Hailey shakes her head.

"Rowan, do you have plans with family for Thanksgiving?" Hailey asks out of nowhere. Thanksgiving's a month away. By then I hope to have my condo deposit back and hopefully a win in small claims court. I could be well on my way, back in the city. Though the holidays aren't a great time to move.

Maybe I could stay here a little longer? No, I've imposed on Mackenzie and Harper enough. And I want to be sure I'm doing what's right for me, not changing my life to spend more time with Cooper. It's not even a relationship. It's fun, casual. Sexy. *Don't think about that.*

A Campbell family Thanksgiving, huh? I think of my ex, my dead mom and grandmom, my estranged dad and brother. God, my family sucks.

I attempt a smile. "I usually go to my friend Meg's celebration in the city. She invites all her friends who don't have families."

"You don't have family?" Hailey asks in horror. "Wait, what about—"

Cooper intervenes. "Mom, that's personal."

"No, it's fine," I say. "Dead, dead, estranged. I'm well used to it."

"You have to come to ours," Hailey says. "We all go to my dear friend Claire Jordan's house."

"More like an estate," Josh says.

"There's room for everyone," Hailey says.

That's right. Harper's mom is Claire Jordan the movie star.

"I wouldn't want to intrude on a family event," I say.

"I insist," Hailey says.

"Yeah, I insist too," Mackenzie says.

"Up to you," Cooper says. "But I do need to mention there's a whole table full of pie."

I smile for real this time. "Thank you. I'd love to go."

Hailey's smile lights up her face. "Good. It'll be so nice to have you. Cooper, this is the kind of woman I've always wanted for you."

Mackenzie laughs.

"Mo-om," Cooper says.

"We're not—" I start.

"We're friends," he finishes.

I point at him. "Exactly."

"Friends to lovers is my favorite story," Hailey says dreamily.

"This isn't one of your Happy Endings Book Club stories," Cooper says. "This is real life."

"Happy Endings Book Club?" I ask.

Hailey beams. "Yes. It's a long-standing romance book club. You're welcome to join us any time."

"Oh, I don't think romance is for me," I say. "I'm sort of in the *never get involved ever again* camp at the moment."

Cooper gestures toward me. "Exactly. She just broke up with her fiancé. Timing is bad for anything love related. Moving on."

Hailey smiles serenely. "Of course. Can you and Rowan get the dessert? It's cherry pie and ice cream."

Cooper stands, so I do too. Mackenzie snickers. Her mom hushes her.

When we get into the kitchen, he says, "Sorry about that. She's always been in love with love. Nothing personal."

He's close again, and I'm lit up inside. My heart's not willing, but my body is. "No, of course I would never take it personally. I'm sure she has lots of women she hoped you'd be with."

"Actually, no."

"Oh."

"But it's cool or whatever. Where is that pie?"

We reach for it at the same time. "Sorry," we say in unison.

"I'll get the pie," I say. "You get the ice cream."

He pulls out vanilla ice cream. "Store bought, not the good stuff. We should stop by Shane's Scoops after this."

"I can't eat two desserts."

"You're not going to be able to go back to this stuff."

"Try me."

He opens the lid, grabs a spoon, and feeds it to me. Our gazes lock.

"It's good," I say.

His thumb brushes my lower lip. "But not great." And then he kisses me, and it's better than great. It's phenomenal.

"Don't forget extra napkins," Hailey calls.

We jerk apart like guilty teenagers.

"Let's get outta here," he says.

I nod.

He grabs the pie and ice cream and sets it on the dining room table. I follow, wondering how he's going to explain our departure.

"Rowan's got a headache," he says. "I'm going to take her home."

"Aww, do you want to take something for it?" Hailey asks.

"Check our medicine cabinet," Mackenzie says.

Finn smirks. Josh raises his brows.

I rub my temple, attempting to fake a headache. "Thanks, but I'd better go lie down." Finn elbows Mackenzie. Her eyes widen in understanding. "And thank you for dinner."

"Bye," Cooper says.

He strides to the door, and I hurry to keep up with him. As soon as we get through the front door, we burst out laughing.

"I think only your mom bought it," I say.

He grabs my hand and walks toward the car. "Who cares? We deserve a little fun."

"Just casual."

"Right. No pressure. No expectations."

"Deal."

We smile at each other. A bubbly feeling rises up in me. I'm happy. And I have a feeling I'm about to be ecstatic.

12

With all the built-up sexual tension between us, I'm expecting a rushed deal, hard thrusts against the wall or a quick tumble into bed. But when we arrive in his bedroom, Cooper stops, his brown eyes searching mine.

I wrap my arms around his neck. "I'm ready."

His gaze drifts to my mouth and lower to my neck. Finally, he cradles my cheek in his large hand and kisses me. A tender kiss that makes my knees week. His hand slides to the back of my neck while his other arm wraps around my waist, holding me as he kisses me deeply. I almost feel…cherished. My limbs feel heavy.

He kisses me like he has all night, on and on, until my entire body softens. A slow burn of desire.

His mouth trails to my jawline to the sensitive spot under my ear. I gasp. I've never been so sensitive. I pull his shirt from his waistband and slide my hands underneath, reveling in the warm muscular planes of his back. Suddenly I need more. Skin on skin.

His breath runs hot over my ear as he whispers, "I want you so bad."

I grab his head and kiss him passionately. I'm ready for the sexy part. I've never been more ready. The kiss turns urgent, igniting me. His fingers spear through my hair in a tight grip, his other hand on the small of my back, pressing me close against his hard body.

He shifts to my neck, hot kisses raining down the column of my throat all the way to my collarbone, his tongue tracing the dip between my collarbones. My pulse jumps.

I step back, pulling my sweater off and letting it drop to the ground. His gaze turns hungry, taking me in. And then his hands frame my face, and he kisses me again. This time more urgent, demanding. Finally, his hands start to roam, skating up my sides to my back, where he expertly undoes my bra. Now I'll experience the quick hookup.

I grab his shirt and pull it over his head. Whoa. I don't think I've ever seen such a gorgeous sexy man in real life. His shoulders are broad, tapering to a trim waist. Pecs and defined abs lead to a V that ends in his jeans. He pulls me against him, and the pleasure of skin on skin makes me want to purr.

He cups my jaw, slowly leaning down to kiss me. I'm no longer in a hurry, reveling in the pace he sets. I fall into the kiss like a soft sigh, a dizzying tumble into deeper kisses that turn me to utter mush. He goes slow, savoring. No man has ever taken their time like this with me.

He drops to his knees and cups one breast, flicking his tongue across my beaded nipple. I arch, aching for more, and he sucks deep. Desire rushes through me, making me weak with need.

"Cooper," I whisper, stroking the soft hair at the nape of his neck.

He gives the other breast the same attention, and my breath comes harder, desire spiking.

I pull him up and unbutton his jeans. He stills my hands. "First, you."

He slowly undresses me, his lusty gaze making me feel like the most desirable woman in the world. His mouth trails down my stomach, and then he kneels to drop a kiss over my sex. The breath whooshes from my lungs as I realize his intention.

His hands cup my ass as he kisses me intimately, his tongue parting me. *Oh my God.* I glance down at his dark head, his hot mouth, his hands firm on me. Within minutes I'm rocking against him, pleasure flooding me, turning me into a mindless, throbbing, aching bundle of need. I pant, my fingers tangling in his hair, and then it hits hard, an explosion of pleasure that makes me cry out. He stays with me, letting me ride out wave after wave of pure pleasure.

He stands and scoops me up in his arms, carrying me to his bed. "You're so sexy."

I sigh. "You're the most amazing man I've ever met." I stiffen, immediately wanting to take the words back. This is supposed to be fun and casual. No pressure, no expectations.

"Thank you. You're amazing too."

I meet his eyes, shocked by the tenderness there. "You don't have to say it just because I said it. I understand this is a onetime thing."

He sets me on the bed and strips out of the rest of his clothes. "It's whatever we want it to be."

Holy crap, he's hung. I didn't expect that. My mouth goes dry.

"I'll be gentle," he says, reaching for a condom from the nightstand.

I'm speechless. It's just wow. He's magnificent.

He rips the foil packet open and rolls it on. Then he covers me with his body, his hand cupping my face. "How're you doing?"

I wrap my arms and legs around him. "Great!"

He smiles. "Good." He shifts, settling between my legs as he slowly slides inside, filling me. He gazes into my eyes. My breath catches, my heart pounding. Because that look is not casual. That look is deep, intimate.

He kisses me, stroking the hair back from my face. My heart cracks open in that moment, a terrifying rush of emotion I'm not ready for.

I lift my hips. "Go hard. I need it." *So I'm not mistaking sex for love.*

I'm rewarded with a hard thrust. I wrap my legs higher around him, taking him deeper. His fingers tangle in my hair as he sucks on the side of my neck and continues with a slow in and out.

"Harder, faster," I urge.

"Slower, deeper," he says in a strained voice, doing exactly that. He slides a hand under my ass and holds me in place for a crazy slow grind of pleasure.

He gazes into my eyes, and I'm caught, drowning in all I feel for this amazing man. I'm too open, too vulnerable, and I can't survive another broken heart.

I grab his ass and pull him hard against me.

And then I cling to him as his control finally snaps and he pounds into me, his breath harsh and hot near my ear. *Yes, yes, yes.* This is what I need. Just two bodies racing to release. I'm lost in sensation, the deep pressure in my core, the heat and strength of him, his scent, and then I tumble over into a powerful release, an explosion of electric pleasure that radiates through my body. He groans with one last deep thrust, shuddering and then stilling.

A long moment later, he rolls off me and heads to the bathroom, probably to get rid of the condom. I'm so limp and boneless, but I know I have to go. That's how friends with benefits works, right? I don't know the rules. I've never done this before. Do I say goodbye? Thank you? Maybe a text once I'm safely home and out of danger of losing my heart to him.

He returns before I can work out the right thing to do. He smiles, and I melt. No, not good. I have to get out of here. I shift to the edge of the bed.

He looks at me over my shoulder. "Stay the night."

"I don't think that's what friends with benefits do."

He pulls me gently to the mattress so I'm lying on my back. "We can do whatever we want. No rules, no pressure, no expectations."

"Well, we should have at least one rule, like sex is just a onetime amazing thing."

He brushes my hair back from my face. "If you stay the

night, it can be more than once, but it'll still count as one time since you never left."

I give in, wrapping my arms around his neck. "You're brilliant."

He kisses me tenderly, settles the covers over me, and shifts me so we're spooning. I love spooning. I hardly ever got a chance to revel in it before. I have a feeling he could do this for hours. Slow and easy just like his personality.

The heat of his body relaxes me. I close my eyes, my body going limp. I'm nearly asleep when I hear him whisper, "I like you too much."

My heart squeezes because I feel the same way. I pretend I'm asleep, not ready to go there.

Cooper

The next morning I wake feeling alert and alive. I look down at Rowan sleeping. She looks like an angel. I kiss her temple and get out of bed. We kept each other up last night. I'll have to wake her soon so she can get to work. I told myself to keep my distance, but I can't help it. I'm so into her. Hopefully, she didn't hear my confession last night. We agreed to light and casual. She's not ready, and I need to be sure she's choosing to be with me not because I'm helping her but for me.

I decide to surprise her with breakfast from Something's Brewing Café. Nothing beats their coffee and fresh-baked muffins. I make the short drive to the café, get breakfast, and head back. The sun seems brighter, the sky more blue. I whistle to myself and stop short. I'm falling for her. I know what that feels like.

The only way to protect my heart is to get her life to the point where she can leave for a new place in the city or stay because she really wants me. Her small claims court date comes up in a few weeks. If she wins the maximum of ten thousand dollars, she'll be free to go. Between that and the return of her condo deposit, she could pay off her wedding debt *and* get a new apartment in the city. I know exactly who can help with that—Cal Sanders, her dad. I looked him up before. He's a corporate lawyer who always wins. He could demolish a small claims court.

I park in front of my place, look up his number, and call. I know she said she didn't want to get him involved, but he's her best option—free and experienced. Besides, it's the least he can do to help the daughter he practically abandoned after her mom died.

This is my last rescue effort on her behalf, I swear. I'll explain why I did it later. She'll thank me in the end.

Rowan

I wake slowly, confused about where I am. Last night comes back to me in a flood of memories and sensations. Cooper and I were all over each other for most of the night. I jackknife upright. What time is it?

Shit. I have twenty minutes to get home, shower, and go to work. I can't be late. I'm new and already messed up in my early days there. Why in the world did I spend the night? Cooper proved too hard to resist with his promise of one night counting as one time. I grab my clothes from around the room and quickly get dressed.

I rush out to the living room just as he returns holding a take-out tray of two coffees and a bag of what's probably delicious baked goods. If this is what friends with benefits is like, I should've tried it out long ago.

"Morning," he says. "Brought you the best coffee in the world and your choice of blueberry or chocolate-chip muffin."

My throat tightens. He's thoughtful, sweet, and a very generous lover. I tingle just remembering last night. "Thank you. Chocolate. I'll need to take it to go. I'm so late."

He gives me a soft smile that melts my heart. "No problem." He takes out his muffin and hands me the bag and my coffee. Our fingers brush with the exchange, sending heat through me.

I meet his warm brown eyes, and all good sense goes out the window. "Friends with benefits can be more than one time, right?"

He cradles my cheek and kisses me before gazing into my eyes. "It can be whatever we want it to be."

My entire body wants to sway into him, to merge once more. If I weren't holding coffee and a muffin, I'd be tearing his clothes off.

I take a step back, worried about how strong the attraction is, how much I long to stay.

It's okay. It's just sex with a friend, right? Nothing to be scared of.

I turn and hurry out the door.

13

I speedwalk to work with my breakfast and make it there just as Hailey's unlocking the front door. Oh, thank God.

"Morning!" she calls cheerfully.

"Morning."

"Oh, looks like you stopped by Something's Brewing Café. They're the best. If you're here in the winter, you have to try their hot cocoa with handmade marshmallows. To die for."

I follow her inside. "That sounds amazing." Part of me wants to stay. The saner part says staying would get me in too deep with Cooper. My heart's not ready for another devastation.

"What did you get?"

I go to my desk and set breakfast there. "Chocolate-chip muffin."

"Those were always Cooper's favorite."

I took his favorite. Now he's stuck with healthy blueberry. Another sweet gesture on top of a sweet gesture. I sigh dreamily and take a sip of what tastes like an extraordinary latte.

I boot up the laptop, prepared to dive into marketing for Christmas and New Year's Eve.

"I must say, Rowan, you look like you're glowing. Did you get good news about your condo deposit?"

My cheeks burn. *Oh, just had wild sex all night with your son.* "Not yet. I'm expecting it back in two and a half weeks."

She smiles sweetly. "You must just be happy. Settling in to our wonderful town."

"That must be it." My phone vibrates with a text. I glance down and see it's from Cooper. I turn the phone over.

Time for work. Must look hardworking and efficient.

Hailey stands. "You know, your coffee smells so good, I think I'm going to get some for myself."

"Oh, let me. I'm your assistant."

"Thank you, Rowan. I'll take a hazelnut latte."

I nod, stuff my phone in my purse, and head out with my own coffee in hand. As soon as I get to the front porch, I check my phone.

Cooper: *I'm off on Wednesday. Stop by when you're done work.*

That's three days away. Not too long to wait, not so intense as seeing each other again the next day. I smile and text back: *See you then.*

Has Cooper done this friends-with-benefits thing before? He's very good at it.

Cooper

Rowan shows up at my door a little after five on Wednesday. She must've come here straight from work. Her blue eyes look lusty as she takes me in. I go hard instantly. *Slow it down. Don't want to scare her.*

"Are you hungry?" I ask.

She wraps her arms around my neck. "Only for you."

I scoop her up, kick the door closed, and carry her to the bedroom. We can get dinner after. It's what the lady wants, and I aim to please.

She strips out of her clothes. "This was all I could think about for days. Friends with benefits rocks."

My throat goes dry. Now I'm the one taking her in with

lusty eyes from her perky breasts to the gentle curve of her sides and the flare of her hips. Unbelievably sexy.

She grabs my shirt and pulls it off. I help her. She reaches for my jeans, and I push her hands away, doing it myself. I have to ease out of them with the bulge I've got going on.

"Take me against the wall," she says. "I've never done that."

"Yeah? We can do whatever you want."

"I'll have to Google some positions for us."

I bite back a laugh. "Or we could just have fun and see what happens."

"I'll give you everything you secretly desire too."

The words snap my control. I close in on her, wrapping an arm around her waist and backing her into the wall. I'm suddenly ravenous for her. My pulse thrums through my veins.

I entwine my fingers with hers and pin her hands against the wall. Her breath comes harder; her eyes dilate. I want her more than I've ever wanted anyone in my life.

"Kiss me," she whispers.

I take her mouth in a passionate kiss, demanding and thorough, pressing my body against her softness. I shift, trailing open-mouthed kisses along the side of her neck, letting my teeth scrape against her. She shivers. I shift lower, kissing along her collarbone to the vulnerable dip by her throat, where her pulse beats rapidly.

"Cooper," she says breathlessly. I love the way she says my name.

I release her hands, kneeling to cup her breast and suck. Her fingers slide into my hair, holding me to her. I switch to the other side, loving the feel of her, the scent; everything turns me on.

I slide a hand between her legs to find her hot and wet and ready. *Slow, slow. Make it good for her.*

She pulls at my shoulders. "Now. Take me now."

I rise to my feet, about to lift her and bury myself deep,

when I belatedly remember the condom. "Touch yourself while I get ready for you."

She frowns. "You're already ready."

I dash to the nightstand and roll the condom on in record time. Then I stride back to her as she stares at my massive erection.

"Oh, that kind of ready," she says.

I lift her, and she wraps her arms and legs around me. She fits me perfectly. She grabs my head and kisses me feverishly. I get in position and push inside just a little.

"More," she demands.

I thrust deep, intense pleasure floods me, and I almost lose it right there. She gasps. I lift her and thrust deep again.

"Yes," she says. "Yes, yes."

I lift her again, reaching between us to stroke her sweet spot. She shudders around me. So good, so damn good. I slow it down, stroking her and thrusting, her every cry and gasp driving me on.

Her nails dig into my shoulders. I can feel her trembling on the edge. I kiss her roughly, swallowing her sexy sounds as I drive into her over and over. She arches her hips, taking me at an angle that sets us both off. I groan into her neck, lost in pleasure.

A moment passes with nothing but the sound of our panting.

I rest my forehead against hers, emotion sneaking in. I want her to be mine. She rests her head on my shoulder and sighs contentedly. I need some distance. It's the only way to keep from making a huge mistake. Friends with benefits is what she wants. We'll see what she chooses when she's back on top of her life.

I lift her chin and kiss her. She smiles dreamily. "Thank you."

I set her back on the floor and hold her by the hips. "Let's go out for dinner."

"We can't go out in public. People will think we're together."

"Why can't friends get dinner together?"

"I haven't been here long, but I've seen enough to know that gossip moves like wildfire through town. We need to keep this secret. That way there's no pressure and no expectations put on us."

I search her expression. Is she really not cool with being seen with me? "I'm not one to sneak around."

"Please? It'll be exciting." She grabs her panties and slides them back on.

"What about tomorrow night at the Halloween party at Happy Endings? Mackenzie said the three of you are going together as the three blind mice."

Her bra goes on. I want her even though I just had her. That's crazy.

"What about it?" she asks.

I huff. "Are you going to pretend you don't know me?"

She puts her hand on my cheek, smiling. "I'm going to pretend I don't know what an amazing lover you are until the coast is clear and I can have my way with you again."

"That sounds okay," I grumble.

"Let's get takeout," she says cheerfully. "I can't spend the night though. I was almost late to work last time."

I almost say I'll set an alarm, but then I realize just how much I want her to spend the night, which is not light and casual at all.

"Sure, whatever," I say.

"Are you mad?"

I spread my palms wide. "I've got a sexy beautiful woman in my bedroom. What's there to be mad about?"

I head to the bathroom and shut the door a little harder than I mean to. I can't believe I'm the one hoping for a relationship. Some real role reversal here. Women always want that from me. Sometimes I feel the same way, sometimes not. But Rowan—I stop myself. She made it clear she wasn't ready.

I just have to wait it out. In three weeks, after her dad

helps win her small claims court case, that's when we'll see how attached to me she really is. Or not.

Rowan

I think Cooper's upset about something. Then I remember we're not in a relationship, so I relax and finish getting dressed.

The bathroom door whips open. He glances at me and then grabs his clothes and gets dressed. Someone should make a sculpture or painting of his muscular naked body. I would stare at it all day.

He walks toward me, looking serious. I gulp. He gives me a quick kiss and steps back. "You should go."

It's like a splash of cold water in the face. "Why?"

"Boundaries. Best not to get too attached."

Hurt, I turn away. "Right. Casual."

He turns my face back toward his. "That's what we agreed on."

I scowl. Way to ruin a great after-sex buzz. I thought we were going to get takeout and hang out. He can't wait to get me out the door. "Right. See ya at the party."

I stride to the front door, open it, and Cooper's hand shoots out, shutting it. I can feel his heat at my back. Every nerve ending tingles in anticipation. He's going to ask me to stay.

His voice is gravelly by my ear. "You forgot your purse."

I turn and grab my purse. "Thank you," I bite out.

He nods and walks away. Well, I can take a hint. I yank open the door and walk out.

Why does it feel like we just had our first fight?

14

———

"We are so damn cute!" Mackenzie exclaims, showing me and Harper the selfie we just took at home in our three blind mice costumes.

"So damn hot, you mean," Harper says. "Brilliant way to wear a little black dress to a costume party."

"You're very creative," I say. We're also wearing mouse-ear headbands and sunglasses.

"I try," Mackenzie says.

The doorbell rings.

"Must be more trick-or-treaters. I'll get it," Mackenzie says as she hurries for the candy bowl.

"We'll have to put a bowl of candy on the porch before we leave," Harper says. "But not before I snag our favorites for later."

"A woman after my own heart," I say.

Mackenzie appears holding a bouquet of flowers. "It was a flower delivery. Who orders flowers for Halloween? They're not even black."

My heart races. Did Cooper send flowers to apologize for kicking me out after sex last night? He didn't need to do that. No strings.

Mackenzie hands them to Harper. "They're for you."

"For me?" Harper plucks the card out and opens it. She reads it to herself and stares at the flowers.

"Who's it from?" Mackenzie asks. "Does Oliver want a second chance?"

Before I arrived in town, Harper had recently had three dates with a guy she met online, Oliver. There wasn't a fourth date because he ghosted her. She said he was dead to her after that.

"No," Harper says quietly.

"Then who?"

Harper heads to the kitchen. We follow her. She fills a vase with water, takes the wrapping off the flowers, and throws it in the trash can under the sink along with the card. She places the flowers in the vase and arranges them before setting them on the center of the kitchen table. "There. Now we can all enjoy our Halloween flowers. Let's go to the party."

Mackenzie grabs the trash can and pulls the card out. She gasps. "It's from Nathan."

"Who's Nathan again?" I ask.

"He's my business partner," Mackenzie says. "And he's also Harper's archrival."

A rare pink suffuses Harper's cheeks. "He's not an archrival. He's my brother's friend. An old family friend. He's whatever."

"Listen to this." Mackenzie reads from the card. "I heard the way to a woman's heart is through flowers." She puts the card down. "Nathan must be making his move after all these years! What're you going to do?"

"Nothing," Harper says. "I have a boyfriend."

"No, you don't," Mackenzie says.

"For tonight's purposes I do. His name is Oliver."

Mackenzie shakes her head.

Harper puts a palm up. "It's ridiculous. Why would he send this?"

I venture to say the obvious, "He must be into you."

She rolls her eyes. "I completely ignored him at Shayla

and Owen's engagement party. Not one word. Suddenly he sends flowers?"

"Maybe he wants a fresh start with you," Mackenzie says. "You were best friends when you first met."

"When we were little kids. That doesn't count."

Mackenzie shrugs. "Let's go and find out."

Harper freezes. "How about some wine before we go?"

Mackenzie sends me a significant look. Not only is Harper stalling, she's nervous to see Nathan. I can't wait to see how this turns out.

I practically float on the short walk around the corner to Happy Endings mostly because we indulged in an excellent sauvignon blanc while Harper bitched about how annoying Nathan is and how he's death to every party. For me, everything feels right with the world. I'm not worried about the future. I'm not thinking about the past. I'm just enjoying the moment.

We step inside Happy Endings to find a spookily decorated bar and restaurant with cobwebs in the corners and scary zombies hanging from the ceiling. A DJ blasts "Monster Mash."

There's a crowd of costumed people, making it even harder to find a familiar face. I feel someone staring and turn, meeting Cooper's eyes, where he's working behind the bar. I push my sunglasses to the top of my head. He's wearing a boxer's red silk robe, and the belt is loosened enough to expose his gorgeous chest. Desire shoots through me.

He winks and turns to a customer, who just happens to be a sexy bunny. She leans across the bar to show her cleavage.

That's it? He didn't gesture for me to join him. I cross my arms, miffed.

Chill. He's not going to give you his full attention when he's working. And there's no shortage of women flirting with the gorgeous bartender. I can't possibly be jealous because that would imply a relationship when we specifically agreed to be friends with benefits. He kicked me out after sex. That tells me all I need to know about where he stands.

"Who's the guy wearing a grass skirt with the tribal tattoo on his arm?" Harper asks. The guy has his back to us. "He's someone I'd like to fu—no!"

A striking man with dark hair, a stubbled square jaw, and muscles galore turns to face us. He's wearing a grass skirt and sandals. That's it. Mackenzie smiles and waves. She takes a step forward when Harper yanks her back.

"No," Harper says. "Let's check out the back room."

Mackenzie pulls her arm free. "You're being ridiculous. It's not like you're never going to see Nathan again. He works with me, and he goes to half our family events too."

Wow. Nathan looks like a model. And he sent flowers.

I turn to Harper. "What's so bad about Nathan?"

"Yeah, what's so bad about Nathan?" a deep baritone voice asks as he joins us. Up close his eyes are a brilliant blue. He says a quick hello to me and Mackenzie before turning to Harper in question.

She flutters a hand in the air and drops it.

Mackenzie stares at her and turns to Nathan. "I think your flowers made her speechless."

"I need a drink." Harper turns to go.

"Me too," Nathan says.

Harper stops and turns back. "I know what flowers mean."

"What do they mean?" Nathan asks gamely.

Mackenzie sneaks a picture of them. They don't notice, too busy staring into each other's eyes. There's definitely something between them. The attraction is palpable, as is the animosity, though I think it's only coming from Harper.

She lifts her chin. "Hope you know this isn't happening. I'm with someone. Oliver is everything to me."

Nathan frowns. "Oliver. That's the first I've heard of him."

"Guess word hasn't gotten out yet."

"Look, I just wanted to make peace for whatever I did that made you mad at me."

"I'm not mad at you."

"Yes, you are."

"No, I'm not."

He cocks his head. "Then why do I feel like you see me as death to the party whenever we cross paths?"

I stifle a laugh. That's exactly what Harper called him.

Harper shrugs.

Nathan gets irritated. "For God's sake, Harper, we grew up together. Is this still about—"

"When did you get that tattoo?" she asks quickly.

He flexes his bicep impressively. "You like it?"

She can't take her eyes off it. "Just curious."

"It's fake to go with the costume."

She backs up a step. "Of course. That makes much more sense. Nothing's changed." She whirls and walks right into me.

"Ow."

"Sorry. Let's go to the back room now."

She darts away. Mackenzie and I follow behind but get caught up in the crowd, slowing us down.

"So that's Nathan," I say to Mackenzie.

"He's loyal, not bad to look at, and smart," Mackenzie says. "Of course she hates him."

"That didn't look like hate to me."

"Those flowers threw her for a loop. Funny thing is, she once told me that tattoos were not sexy. Anyone could get one. Yet she couldn't keep her eyes off it."

"What happened to make her so mad at him?" I ask.

"I think it's more what didn't happen. I suspect she either made a pass at him and he turned her down, or worse, they hooked up and he ignored her after. She refuses to talk about it."

"Or she's madly in love with him, and she's indulging in a frenemy war like your parents."

Mackenzie bursts out laughing. "Right. Mom wasn't

madly in love with Dad when that went down. Who knows what goes on in Harper's mind? She's complicated."

"Aren't we all?"

We pass the bar on the way to the back room. Cooper's in deep conversation with a beautiful redheaded woman wearing a maid costume. He doesn't even notice me.

"Hi, Cooper!" I yell. "Nice costume."

He gives me a small smile and goes back to chatting with the redhead.

Jerk. Just because I said we couldn't go out in public together doesn't mean we can't speak to each other in public. Or maybe he's just trying to respect the line I drew. Part of me wants to push that line. Just a little.

Mackenzie and I continue on.

"So what's going on with you and Cooper?" Mackenzie asks when we reach the back room.

I wave madly. "There's Harper. We'd better save her. Big Foot looks like he's making a move."

When we reach her, Harper's in a heated debate over the existence of Big Foot with the guy dressed as Big Foot. She says he's not real, and this guy truly believes. He even pulls his phone out to show her pictures of what really does look like sightings of Big Foot.

An old woman wearing a flapper costume starts a conga line, and we get swept up in it. I laugh as we move our way past the pool table and an old-fashioned jukebox. She leads us out of the room past the bar, and I slip away, taking a seat on a barstool. It's my turn to talk to Cooper. For once he's talking to a guy. A handsome guy in his twenties with brown hair and brown eyes, wearing a mechanic's jumpsuit.

Wait a minute. I know him. He's the guy from *Hot Finds!* "Are you Mason Shaw?"

He gives me a slow, sexy smile. "Sure am. Are you a fan?"

Cooper clears his throat. "Rowan, this is my cousin Mason. He's the one who lent us a truck to move your stuff."

I smile. "Thanks for that. It's so great to meet you in person. You're, like, famous or something."

Mason chuckles. "Aunt Claire is famous. I'm just a mechanic."

"Real original costume," Cooper says.

Mason gives his shoulder a shove and turns back to me. "Hey, you want a drink?"

"I'll get it." Cooper's dark eyes smolder into mine. "I know what she likes."

Mason looks between us. "Sorry, man. I didn't know you two had a thing."

"We do," I say. "We have a thing."

Cooper smiles. "We do?"

"Yeah."

He leans across the bar and kisses me. "I get off at midnight. Meet me here."

"Oh, it's like that," Mason says with a knowing look.

I gaze into Cooper's eyes, affection bursting through me. "Something like that."

"Time for the costume contest," the DJ announces.

"Where's our third blind mouse?" Mackenzie yells.

Cooper whistles, and she hurries over. She looks between us and sighs. "Cooper."

"It's good. No worries, sis."

"Come on," she says to me.

I follow her to the main dining area for the costume contest. "What was that about with Cooper?"

"I told him not to get involved with you. Nothing personal. The last woman he rescued dumped him as soon as he got her life back in order. Besides, you're not serious about him, are you? How could you be so soon after your wedding and life imploded. It's a rebound situation. I just don't want him to get hurt again."

"I don't want to get hurt again either. That's why we're being careful."

She lifts one shoulder. "Well, it's his heartbreak. He's a grown man. Nothing against you. It's just not ideal, you know?"

"I know."

Harper grabs our arms and pulls us into the line to show off our costumes for the judges. I tell myself not to worry about future heartbreak because things are great with Cooper just as they are.

"Sunglasses," Mackenzie says, elbowing me.

I put my sunglasses on. "I won't hurt your brother."

"I know you won't mean to," Mackenzie says. "But what's going to happen when you get your condo deposit back and you move back to the city? You'll get caught up in life there."

I almost say we'll stay in touch, but I can't guarantee that. We're light and casual. Just having fun.

I look over to the bar, where Cooper's laughing with Mason. My heart thumps harder. I can't wait to have more fun when he gets off work.

The moment I get into Cooper's car, we reach for each other, kissing passionately. I can't get enough of him.

I pull away. "I won't hurt you. Mackenzie's afraid I will, but I'll be careful."

"My sister needs to mind her own business."

"As long as we're one hundred percent honest with each other, no one gets hurt. Like, if you want to go out with one of the women you meet at the bar, like that maid or the bunny, that's okay. Just tell me."

He strokes my hair back from my face, an amused look on his face. "Rowan, I don't want a maid or a bunny. You know I make money with tips, right? I'm friendly to everyone."

"Right, right. But if you did want to be with someone else, just let me know, no hard feelings."

"I don't want you to be with someone else. I want you all to myself."

"I don't want to be with anyone. I only made an exception for you because you're so…"

"Sexy?" He flexes both arms. "Strong?" He winks. "Charming?"

"Good. Because you're so good."

He throws his head back dramatically. "Not the good-guy label. That's the guy you keep in the friend category."

I rub his chest under his boxer robe. "You're the sexiest friend I've ever had. Now can we please go back to your place so I can show you what I do with my sexiest friend?"

He starts the car, puts it in gear, and peels out of the lot. "I like your style."

"I like you. A lot."

He glances at me, a smile tugging at the corners of his lips. "Yeah?"

I nod.

He takes my hand, entwining our fingers together. I'm happy. I'm actually happy. As long as I don't think about the future, I can revel in the magic of Cooper.

15

———

Cooper

Three weeks go by in a blur of sexy times and lots of laughs. Dare I say Rowan is happy? I know I am. We spend every Sunday together all day and night. She's a regular at Sunday family dinner. They all love her. Wednesday nights we have dinner at my place, and she spends the night. When I'm working, she shows up on her lunch break to have lunch with me in the kitchen at Happy Endings.

I can't deny my feelings any more, but I keep it to myself. Tomorrow Rowan goes to small claims court. If she wins, like I think she will with her dad's help, then I'll know if she chooses me or her old life.

My gaze collides with hers the moment she walks into Happy Endings. She just got off work. She beams at me, and my heart kicks harder.

She goes up to the bar, leans across it, and kisses me. She's not as worried about people knowing about us. A good sign.

"How'd it go today at love central?" I ask.

"Pretty good. I feel like I'm really contributing now, you know?"

I incline my head. "I'm sure you are. So you think you might want to stay on there permanently?"

"I'm not sure. The thing I like best is the online marketing and social media, so maybe I should do that instead with my own business, and Love Junkies could be one of my clients."

"Working from Clover Park?"

"Well, I suppose that's a possibility with remote work, but since I'm starting from scratch, I'd probably have more luck picking up big clients if I was networking in the city. I got my condo deposit back, so I could move back now."

"Okay."

"But the holidays are coming up. It might not be the best time to move, you know?"

Hope sneaks in. "Sure. Thanksgiving, Christmas, New Year."

"I asked Mackenzie and Harper if I could stay through the end of November since I'm going to your family's Thanksgiving. They said I can stay as long as I like."

I take her hand. "Sounds like you found your place here."

"I'm comfortable, but am I giving up bigger opportunities in the city?"

"Are you happy?"

She considers that and then smiles. "I am." She laughs. "If you had told me six weeks ago that I'd be happy living in a small town, working for a wedding planner, and dating a guy who works at a place called Happy Endings, I would've thought you were nuts."

I kiss her palm. "So we're dating now? Moving beyond friends with benefits?"

"I think we both know we've moved beyond."

"How can you tell?"

She leans close to whisper, "Because I miss you when I can't be with you."

"That's a good reason." I kiss her. "Me too."

~

Rowan

I sit on the bench outside the courtroom, reviewing what

I'm going to say. I feel good about my chances in there. I found a picture of Mom wearing the jewelry, and I have a receipt for my laptop and noise-cancelling headphones. I'm not sure the value of the jewelry, but a pearl necklace and diamond earrings have to be worth something. Dad bought them for her as Christmas gifts. He had the money to get something nice.

I hear my name. It's my turn to go into the courtroom. Nerves skitter through me as I walk in and take a seat near the front, waiting to be called before the judge. Only a handful of people are in here. I guess they hear several cases in a day.

The door bursts open in the back of the courtroom. A man in a navy suit strides down the aisle like he owns the place. He's in his fifties, salt-and-pepper hair. *Dad? What's he doing here?*

He nods to the judge and sits next to me, leaning close to whisper, "I'm here to represent you."

"How did you know I was here?"

"Your friend Cooper Campbell called me."

I clench my teeth. All the time I've spent with Cooper and he didn't think to mention he called my dad behind my back? I told him Dad and I aren't on good terms. How could he do this?

He probably thought he'd rescue me once again. Well, guess what? I was down before, but I got back up. Dammit. I let my feelings for him cloud my judgment. I got comfortable in town with him, with his family.

I can't believe he did this!

Then, to my further shock, Dave walks in, dressed casually. I was sure he wouldn't show and drag this case out further. He lifts a hand in a small wave toward me. I face front.

A guy on the other side of the row is called to state his case.

Dad pulls a folder from his briefcase. "This is the first time I've done pro bono work."

I keep my voice low, but inside I'm seething. "Pro bono? So I'm a charity case."

"Semantics."

"I don't need your help. They told me I can represent myself. That guy is." I gesture toward the guy up front.

Dad doesn't bother to reply. He never was much of a talker unless it was for work.

"I'll tell the judge you don't represent me," I say.

"Don't be foolish. I'll get you the full amount. I brought my original receipts for the jewelry. It's only appreciated in value."

I press my lips in a flat line. Part of me wants to kick him out; part of me says let the man do what he's best at. "Fine."

After a quick judgment for two hundred dollars to the guy before me for an overdue cable bill, it's my turn.

I walk up to the microphone. Dad joins me. Strangely, it makes me more confident to have a lawyer by my side, even if it is the man I have a complicated relationship with.

I state my case and that Dad is representing me. "I have receipts for the stolen laptop and headphones. My ex-fiancé, David Phillips, sitting over there, has admitted to hocking them after we broke up."

Dad pulls the microphone toward him. "Your Honor, I'd like to present receipts for the stolen jewelry's value."

Dave hangs his head. He was probably going to claim the jewelry wasn't worth anything.

But when it's Dave's turn to defend himself, he goes with, "I never touched her stuff."

I tell the judge the whole story of what he's done, Dad tops it off with some precedent in a domestic dispute I've never heard of, and the judge bangs her gavel.

The judge gives Dave a hard look. "Civil money judgment on David Phillips for the maximum of ten thousand dollars. An enforcement officer will be assigned to you. See the clerk on your way out."

Dave slinks out.

"Yes," I say under my breath. I want to yell it, but we're in a courtroom. I turn to Dad. My impulse is to hug him for hanging on to those receipts and helping me out today. But I can't. This is the same man who left me with only Mom's jewelry to hang onto.

He gives me a curt nod. "Congratulations."

"Thank you."

We file down the aisle and out the door. I'm expecting him to rush off to work, but he says, "Rowan, can we talk for a minute outside?" He sounds uncertain like he's afraid I'll reject him.

"Okay."

A few minutes later, we're outside. There's a fountain in the plaza out front, and we walk over to it.

Dad folds his hands in front of him. "Your friend Cooper would've made a fine lawyer. He laid out his points clearly with exactly what he expected me to do to make things right with you."

I shake my head. "He had no right. I didn't ask him to do any of that."

Dad holds my gaze, his blue eyes so like my own. "I didn't think of it as abandoning you when I sent you to live with your grandmother. I thought I did what was best for you. You needed a woman in your life. I…" His voice chokes. My eyes widen. I've never seen him emotional. Even at Mom's funeral, he kept a stoic expression. "I was consumed with grief and threw myself into work. Success was a lonely hard road. I have regrets, especially where they concern you."

"Oh my God, are you dying?"

"No, I'm just trying to say I should've tried harder to connect with you, and I'm sorry for abandoning you. You were grieving as much as I was."

My throat tightens. It's the apology I never thought I would get. "I don't know what to say."

"I'd like to spend more time with you now, if it's not too late."

Tears sting my eyes. "Oh, Dad, it's not too late."

He opens his arms to me, and I hug him.

We pull apart. He wipes his eyes from tears. Wow. That must've been hard for him to say. He clears his throat like he's embarrassed. "I'm going to hire a private detective to track down your jewelry. It's your legacy."

"Thanks, Dad."

We stand there awkwardly for a moment.

"Would you like to have lunch with me?" he asks. "My treat."

I smile. "Sure."

We walk down the street together, heading to a new beginning.

~

On the train ride home, I consider next steps. I have my condo deposit back, and the money Dave owes me will eventually get to me. Dad told me there's ways to make sure I get that money, and he'll stay on it. So now I have options. I don't have to stay in Clover Park, working for Hailey, living with Mackenzie and Harper, seeing Cooper. Dammit, Cooper, why did you have to make things so complicated?

I fell for him, even though I tried my best not to get sucked in. And then he had to go behind my back, bringing Dad into this. How can I trust Cooper not to do something like that again? He'll think he's helping, but really he's treating me like a woman in need of rescue. It doesn't matter that it worked out with Dad. Cooper broke my trust.

Is it time I left Clover Park? My mind flashes to memories of my time there: dinner with Mackenzie and Harper, watching our favorite mystery show and yelling at the screen, little Felix always wanting to be in my lap. Shane's Scoops with the best ice cream in the state. Hailey with her warm vibrant personality, cheering my efforts on, inviting me to Sunday family dinner.

I love working with her. I've been seriously considering asking if I could stay in a permanent position there. It seems like there's room for me to grow. Maybe even be an equal partner in the business one day.

And then there's Cooper. Wonderful Cooper, who's been everything I didn't know I wanted. But he crossed the line. Big time.

If I leave Cooper, the rest goes away too. They're his family; they'll side with him.

I exhale sharply. I have to do what's best for me in the long run.

16
———

My stomach drops. "What do you mean you're breaking up with me?"

Rowan and I are in the back office of Happy Endings for this private conversation. She walked into the bar with a solemn expression, and I knew right away it couldn't be good news. I thought maybe she'd lost the case, but she won. Everything worked out, yet she's dumping me.

Her chin lifts. She's standing close in the small space, but she's never felt farther away. "I mean I can no longer trust you, so it's over."

I sit on the edge of the desk and pat the space next to me. "Let's talk about this. Tell me why you can't trust me." I'm grasping at straws because, even though I knew winning the case would give her the option to leave, I hadn't thought through how hard it would be if she did. My gut churns.

She remains standing. "You called my dad behind my back, knowing he abandoned me and we have, like, zero relationship, and had him represent me today."

"But you won. Isn't that the most important thing?"

"Why didn't you tell me?"

I throw my hands up. "Because I knew you would call him off, and I wanted you to win."

She shakes her head. "I trusted you, and you know how hard that is for me to do after Dave."

"You can still trust me, I swear."

"Right. Just like I trusted Dave, and look how great that turned out. I knew it was a mistake to get involved with someone so soon."

"The timing wasn't great, but what we have is real."

She's quiet for a long painful moment. "I'm getting the full settlement of ten thousand dollars. Dad and I had lunch together—"

"That's great."

"But none of that matters between you and me. I can't be worrying constantly about what you're doing behind my back."

I swallow hard. "Does this mean you're leaving Clover Park?"

"I have to, don't I? Everyone I know here is because of you. Your family won't want to have me around once they know you and I aren't together anymore."

"They'll treat you just the same. They like you for you. Don't blow up your life here because you're mad at me."

"I'm not mad, I'm hurt." She looks to the ceiling, blinking rapidly. "You broke my already fragile heart."

I reach for her. "Rowan, I'm sorry."

She pulls away, shaking her head. "Bye." She slips out the door.

I sit there for a long devastating moment. Rowan did exactly what Brianna did to me. I fixed her life, and she dumped me. I knew better.

I scrub a hand over my face. Dammit all to hell. I miss Rowan already.

Rowan

It's time to untangle my life from Cooper's. I go to Ludbury House and find Hailey in her office.

"Hi, Hailey."

She jumps up. "Hi! I wasn't expecting you to come in today. How did it go in court?"

"I won."

"That's great!" She steps closer, studying my expression. "Why don't you seem happy?"

A lump of emotion clogs my throat. "I, uh, guess it's been a stressful day. I won the full amount, best I could've hoped for. I'll give you a large payment toward my wedding."

"We can stick to our payment plan. You'll need that money."

"And I need to resign."

"Why?"

"Because I'm going back to the city."

"Did you get a new job?"

"No."

"Did something happen with Cooper?"

My face crumples. "I need to go."

"Honey, I can see you're upset. Stay and talk about it. I'm sure together we can come up with a solution."

"You're his mom. You can't be objective."

"Okay, you don't have to talk to me. How about Mackenzie?"

"His sister?"

"Harper."

I blow out a breath. "This town is filled with people who are either related to Cooper or friends or adoring fans."

"What do you mean adoring fans?"

I wave briskly. "You know, all the other women he rescued who constantly come into the bar and hang all over him."

"Rowan, he's in love with you. I know my son. He's never been so happy before."

I stare in shock for a moment. In love with me? He never said he was in love with me. It's too soon for big heavy emotions that can devastate you.

"I have to go." I turn and then turn back, giving her a fierce hug. "Thanks for everything."

I hurry out the door, but I still hear her say, "I'll miss you."

Tears blur my eyes as I leave. I have to go home and pack. Where is home? I don't even know anymore.

It doesn't take long to pack up my room. I'll have to hire movers to get my furniture out of Harper's she-shed later. My friend Meg said I could crash with her at her apartment in the city. Yes, it'll be crowded with her roommates, but if I don't leave now, I never will.

Mackenzie's downstairs working on her laptop. Harper went out for pizza. As soon as she gets back, I'll break the news that I'm leaving.

I head downstairs, and Felix darts between my legs, nearly tripping me. I catch myself on the railing, my heart racing. That would've been a long flight of stairs to tumble down. "I can't tell if you love me or you're trying to kill me."

He reaches the bottom before I do and walks off with a puffy tail shaking in the air. Guess he got freaked as much as I did by my tripping on him.

"Pizza's here!" Harper announces.

Mackenzie sets her laptop aside. "Great, I'm starving. Did you get peppers and mushrooms?"

"I got peppers. No mushrooms because mushrooms are gross."

Mackenzie turns to me. "Do you think mushrooms are gross?"

"No."

"They're fungi," Harper says, heading to the kitchen. "Enough said."

We follow her.

Mackenzie gets out plates and napkins. I get sparkling water for Mackenzie and pour tap water for Harper. I know what they like.

I join them at the table but don't take a slice of pizza.

"You're not hungry?" Harper asks.

My stomach growls in response. I press a hand to it. "I need to tell you ladies something."

They both stare at me. "What is it?" they say in near unison.

"I'm going back to the city. Tonight and for good."

"Why?" Mackenzie asks.

"Is this because of Cooper?" Harper asks.

My throat closes. I grab Harper's water and take a sip. "It's just time."

"What did he do?" Mackenzie demands.

"Don't dump us just because my cousin pissed you off," Harper says.

"It's just…it's time. Thank you for everything."

"Wait! Where are you going?" Mackenzie asks. "I thought you hadn't found an apartment yet."

"I'm going to stay with my friend Meg while I look for a place."

Harper shoots me an incredulous look. "Meg with the three roommates?"

"Yeah, it'll be fun, like a sleepover."

"One bathroom and two of the roommates are guys," Mackenzie says. "I thought we all agreed that would be disgusting."

"Well, yeah, but…" Felix jumps in my lap. I pet him, finding comfort.

Mackenzie squeezes my arm. "Let's eat, and then we'll talk some more, okay? We're all friends here."

"We really can't help it if we're related to Cooper," Harper says matter-of-factly.

I set Felix down and take a slice of pizza. Mackenzie knocks her pizza slice against mine in a toast. I take a bite, and it's delicious.

~

Two slices and a bottle of wine later, I've agreed to stay the night. Tomorrow's soon enough to start my new life. Mackenzie's telling us a story about a client who was so demanding Nathan wanted to charge them an inconvenience fee.

We laugh, even Harper, who usually scowls just at the sound of his name. We're gathered in the living room now on the cushy sofa under a shared fleece blanket. It's cozy, and I can't help but wish I could bottle this moment.

"So now that we've convinced you to hang around a little longer, do you want to tell us what happened with Cooper?" Mackenzie asks. "Forget he's my brother. This is a sisters-before-misters situation."

Sisters. How I wish I could stay and keep these two in my life. Sure, they could visit me in the city, but it's more than an hour away. They'd get busy; I'd get busy. We'd drift apart.

"Did his hero complex get in the way?" Harper asks. "All you have to do is tell him to stand down."

"That would be hard for him," Mackenzie says. "When it comes to someone he loves, he'll do anything to make sure they're happy."

I suck in air. "You're the second person today to say he's in love with me. He never said that. In fact, he's said repeatedly that what we have is casual, no expectations, no pressure."

"Sweet," Mackenzie says. "He's putting you at ease. All you have to do is look at the two of you together to see you're both madly in love."

My jaw drops. "What! I'm not in love. I just got out of a serious relationship. My heart is shattered. I'm done with…" I trail off. How can I say I'm done with men when I've spent so much time with Cooper? It wasn't just sex. We took day trips together on Sundays, caught meals together while he was working, texted daily.

Mackenzie's right. Cooper acted casual for my sake, to put me at ease. Thinking back to my first Sunday family dinner, Hailey told me he'd never been a player. He cares about me. But love?

Am *I* in love?

How did I let this happen?

Harper elbows me. "Denial only works for so long."

I take them both in. "The thing is, my ex destroyed me. He broke my trust in so many ways. And now Cooper broke my trust. It's the one thing I can't forgive."

"Did he apologize?" Mackenzie asks.

I nod.

"Did he leave you at the altar?" Harper asks.

Mackenzie reaches over me to smack Harper's arm. It's not easy with the blanket. "Your deranged sense of humor is not appreciated."

I fix the blanket over us. "He called my dad behind my back and got him to represent me in small claims court today. I told you how Dad and I aren't close. He dropped me off at my grandmother's after Mom died and barely kept in touch."

Harper cocks her head. "Well, you left out that your dad was in court today. So Dad won the case for you?"

"Yeah."

"Why didn't you tell him to leave?" Mackenzie asks.

"Because he's a lawyer, and he had receipts that proved the value of Mom's jewelry. That's not the important thing. The important thing is Cooper did this behind my back. How can I trust him again? For all I know, he'll keep doing things behind my back, in my best interests, of course, and I'll constantly be blindsided."

"But it worked out," Mackenzie says.

"That's what he said!" I exclaim. "I can't be worrying over what else he's going to do without telling me. It might not have worked out. I could've flipped out, seeing my dad there, kicked him out, represented myself while I was upset, and lost the whole case."

Harper holds up a finger. "What if you did something behind his back in his best interests so he can see what that feels like. Then you can both agree never to do that again."

I shake my head. "That's ridiculous. I made plans to leave. I quit my job at Love Junkies, I already packed my stuff upstairs, and Meg's expecting me tomorrow."

They give me twin looks of skepticism.

"Lame excuse," Harper says.

"Oh, please let us plan something for Cooper," Mackenzie says. "It would be so great to see his reaction. No woman has ever done something for him."

I frown. "No one?"

Mackenzie shakes her head. "His last serious girlfriend, Brianna, paid him back for all he did by bailing on him. She moved to the city."

"Oh, man, he's probably curled in the fetal position over this," Harper says. "Shades of Brianna in your case. Today was the last financial piece you needed to leave, he made sure you got it, and now you're out of here."

My heart aches at the idea of Cooper in a fetal position over the double whammy of his ex and me. He's had heartbreak too. He's all give, give, give. I know something about that.

"Let's give him a taste of his own medicine," I say. "I just thought of something awesome, but it might take a few days to make it happen."

"Ooh, I'm in!" Mackenzie says.

"Time to rescue the dude-in-distress," Harper quips.

We crack up.

17

Cooper

After Rowan left Happy Endings, I wanted nothing more than to go home, punch something, and howl. But I had to work. No way I was going to ask Dad to come in on his day off. He'd think I wasn't taking responsibility, and then who knows how long it would take before he made me partner?

Now it's been a week since Rowan dumped me, and I'm back at Happy Endings for my Saturday shift. I've moved from howling to pissed off. It's all crystal clear now. Women use me and leave. No more Mr. Nice Guy.

My parents appear at the bar, surprising me. "Hey, what're you doing here?"

"Actually," Mom says, barely able to contain her smile, "we're here to give you the day off."

"Don't you have a wedding?" I ask.

"No. The Saturday before Thanksgiving isn't a popular wedding day."

Dad goes behind the bar with me.

Mom waves. "Going to check how things are going in the kitchen. I'm manager today!"

"Why?" I ask Dad.

He points to where Rowan just walked in. "That's why.

She called us and asked if we could take your shift because she has something planned for you."

Right. Probably wants to ask me to help her move into Meg's place.

Rowan comes up to the bar. "Hi." Her voice is soft like she's uncertain of how I'll respond to the fact that she called my parents behind my back while I'm working just so she could ask me for yet another favor. I can clear that up.

"Hi. I don't know why you called my parents, but I'm not leaving."

"You should go," Dad says.

I speak between my teeth. "I don't want to go."

Dad stares me down. "If you don't go, you're fired."

Rowan waves both hands frantically. "No, no, no. Nothing like that. Just please come with me."

"Fine." I walk out from behind the bar and join her. "What?"

"Follow me."

I follow her out the front door, where a group of women stand, each holding identical small wrapped gifts. Hold on. I know these women. I've helped every single one of them. There's Gina, Rachel, Vickie, Samantha, and Kristen. Tall Vickie shifts to reveal my ex, Brianna. The tips of my ears burn. I can't believe Rowan called Brianna to witness whatever this is. She's the worst one of them all, dumping me after her life was back on track.

Brianna's the reason I'm pissed at Rowan for doing the same thing. Only Rowan came back.

"What's this about?" I ask.

Vickie comes forward and hands me a gift. "Thank you for all you did for me. Your efforts have not been wasted, I promise. I pay it forward in every way I can."

I stare at the gift in my hand. "You didn't have to get me anything."

"It's my way of giving back to you."

This is the first time a woman ever gave me something.

Besides family, that is. It's a weird feeling to be on the receiving end of goodwill.

I turn to Rowan in question. She plucks the gift from my hand and sets it on a nearby bench. I turn back to find Gina in front of me.

"Hi, Cooper. You've got a keeper this time. She wouldn't take no for an answer." She hands me a gift. "Thank you."

"You're welcome."

Rowan plucks the gift from my hand as Rachel approaches. Same deal—a gift and a sincere thank you. There's a strange wetness in my eyes.

Next is Samantha, then Kristen, and finally Brianna. I tense. I haven't seen her since the breakup.

She hands me my own shirt—a blue button-down she wore the morning after at my place and took with her. "Sorry about the way things ended. And thank you for all you did for me. I appreciate it more than you know. You gave me hope."

Rowan snatches the shirt from my hand and tosses it over the back of the bench. I turn back to the women, wondering what they'll do next.

"Bye!" they chorus, waving before they walk away.

I relax a little, especially once Brianna goes. I'm over her, but it's still painful to see her again.

I turn to Rowan. "Not thrilled you called my ex behind my back and made all these women thank me and give me gifts."

"But I did it in your best interests. You deserve to be thanked."

"And all Brianna got me was my own shirt back."

"You're better off without her."

I spear a hand through my hair. "Was this some kind of payback because I went behind your back with your dad?"

She gives me a small smile. "At first it was, but then I thought it was about time someone did something for you."

I search her expression, unsure of her intentions.

"Cooper, I don't want to break up. You're the best thing to ever happen to me."

I fold her into my arms, relieved and so thankful. I push her hair back from her face and cradle her cheek. "You're the best thing to ever happen to me too."

"All this time I've been trying to get back to my old life when what I really needed was to build a new life. I've been doing that, bit by bit, but always with one foot out the door. I'm staying for you, for my job at Love Junkies, for my new friends Harper and Mackenzie, and for this wonderful town that's been so welcoming."

"You don't have to give up your dreams for me. If you want to live in the city, I will too. I can commute for work."

"But it's more than an hour commute!"

"You're worth it."

She throws her arms around me. "Oh, Cooper." She pulls back to look at me. "I'm happy here, but it's nice to know you care enough to move for me too."

"I love you." My voice chokes.

"I love you too."

I frame her face in my hands and kiss her tenderly. When I pull away, she wipes tears from her cheeks. She laughs. "Happy tears, I swear. Should we celebrate with ice cream?"

I nuzzle her neck, and she shivers. "I've got a better idea."

She smiles. "I can't wait."

Mom and Dad step outside. I'm instantly embarrassed. How much of this *women gifting me presents* scene did they see? They were probably watching through the large front window.

Mom spreads her hands wide. "Do we have a happy ending?"

Rowan nods. "I'd like to keep my job with you permanently. It seems like there's room to grow. Maybe even be partner one day?"

"I'd love that!" Mom exclaims, giving her a hug. She pulls back, smiling. "Besides, I wasn't going to accept your resignation."

"What do you think's in all these wrapped presents?" Dad asks. "They're about the same size."

"Open one," Rowan says, smiling. I have a feeling she coordinated the gifts too.

I rip open the paper, slide the top off the box, and find tissue paper. Under that is a shot glass with a four-leaf clover on it that says Lucky Shot.

"Ha!" Dad says. "For Clover Park, I get it."

Rowan smiles. "Clover Park is lucky. At least it is for me. I thought you could display it at the bar. Spoiler alert—they're all the same."

Dad tosses me my shirt. Mom gathers the shot glasses. "Go on, you two. Enjoy the day."

"Get outta here," Dad growls and winks at Rowan.

"Bye!" Rowan says happily.

We walk hand in hand, on our way to the next awesome part of our lives. Together.

EPILOGUE

It's the end of December, only a few days away from Owen and Shayla's New Year's Eve wedding, and Cooper and I are on our way to Happy Endings to celebrate Hailey's birthday. She's become like a mom to me, so I'm giving her my mother's pearl necklace. Dad's private detective tracked the jewelry down in a pawnshop and had it returned to me. Once the pawnshop owner found out they were stolen, he gave them up. At least that's the story Dad told me. I'm keeping the diamond earrings for myself. In fact, I'm wearing them tonight. Why save nice things in a drawer? I'm enjoying every day like it's a special occasion.

Cooper pulls into the back lot of Happy Endings. He's wearing a navy suit, no tie, with a white button-down shirt open at the collar. He's so handsome. I'm wearing my favorite little black dress with a lacy black shawl.

He kisses me. "Ready for my family?"

"Of course. I did all right at Thanksgiving, didn't I?"

"You were momentarily starstruck by my aunt Claire, but you recovered nicely."

I crinkle my nose. "Are you sure you just want to give your mom a gift card for her birthday?" He's carrying a birthday card with a gift card inside. I have an actual present that's both beautiful and meaningful. "It *is* your mom."

He kisses my nose. "This way she can get whatever she wants."

"O-kay, if that's how you want to play it."

He laughs, gets out of the car, and helps me out of my side of the car. He's very attentive. Not just with his manners, but he really listens. He values my opinions. He values me. Getting dumped on my wedding day in Clover Park was the best thing to ever happen to me. Who would've thought I'd ever see it that way?

Once we get inside the restaurant, it seems like everyone's already there, dressed nicely for the occasion. Cheerful balloons and streamers decorate the dining area and bar. I spot a hot buffet and waiters circulating with champagne.

"Your mom really knows how to plan an event," I whisper to Cooper.

"Oh, she didn't plan this," he says.

Someone whispers, "They're here." And then several people shush them. My gaze stops on a familiar-looking face. Dad?

I walk over to him. "Hi."

"Cooper invited me," Dad says quickly. "Hope you don't mind. I really wanted to be here for this." He offers his hand to Cooper and shakes it. "Great to meet you."

"You too," Cooper says.

I stare at Cooper, pull him aside, and then whisper fiercely, "You promised not to do stuff behind my back."

"This is a special occasion," he says. "Trust me. Besides, I wanted to meet your family too."

"I do trust you, but it's weird. He doesn't even know your mom."

He points across the room. "Let's go say happy birthday to her."

I follow him to where Hailey stands next to her husband, Josh. "Happy birthday!" I hug her and give her my gift.

"Oh, you didn't have to give me a gift," Hailey says. "Just

working with you is gift enough. I'd like to make you partner in the new year."

I put a hand to my heart, shocked. "So soon?"

"Of course! You've become my right-hand woman. We'll talk strategy in the new year for further growth for the company. You're an entrepreneur at heart just like me."

"Thank you so much!"

I turn to Cooper to see what he thinks of this outstanding turn of events and find him on one knee, holding up a diamond ring. My heart lodges in my throat. I glance around as the family gathers close to witness the momentous event. That's why he invited Dad.

"This isn't a birthday party at all, is it?" I ask.

His warm brown eyes gaze into mine. "No, sweetheart, it isn't."

"Yes!" I exclaim. I've never been more sure of something in my life.

His family laughs. His cousin Rafael, the photographer, zooms in on us for a picture.

"Let me get this out," Cooper says. "Rowan Sanders, the moment we met, I was hooked. You're a woman of grit, smarts, and incredible beauty. I love you more every day and plan to for the rest of my life. Will you marry me?"

Tears leak out of my eyes. I nod. "Yes."

He slides the ring on my finger, rises to his feet, and hugs me tight. Cheers and applause surround us.

I pull back to look at him. "You were very tricky with the birthday party thing. You even bought a birthday card!"

"Oh my goodness!" Hailey exclaims, hurrying over with the pearl necklace I gave her. "Rowan, this is too much."

"It was my mom's. I wanted you to have it because you're more than just my employer and friend. You're like a mom to me."

She hugs me and places the necklace around my neck. "Then this is a gift from mother to new daughter. Welcome to the family, Rowan."

My lower lip trembles. She folds me into her arms, and I

sigh, relaxing. And then everyone's rushing up to congratulate us.

"This is so wonderful!" Mackenzie exclaims, hugging us both at the same time. "Now I've got a sister!"

I give her a watery smile. "I've always wanted a sister!"

Harper hugs me next. "Looks like a taste of his own medicine was exactly what he needed. Congrats to both of you."

"Thank you!" I say.

A waiter stops by to give us both champagne.

Josh raises his glass. "To the happy couple! Congratulations!"

I clink my glass against Cooper's, and then Mackenzie and Harper clink glasses with me too. I take a sip of the bubbly drink.

"We miss our roommate," Harper says to me.

"Aww, I see you guys all the time," I say. I moved in with Cooper last weekend.

"Not the same," she pouts.

"Felix misses you too," Mackenzie says.

"I promise to visit all of you regularly," I say.

"Come see the shot glass display," Cooper says.

I walk with him to the bar, where a new display case holds his Lucky Shot shot glasses. "Very cool."

"I didn't want them to get dusty. People wanted to use them, but I said no. I want to keep them in perfect condition because that's the day when we got together for good."

"Sweet. I love it."

He goes behind the bar. "This is like the first time we met. Me right here, you right there." He gestures to his cousin Rafael, who comes over and takes our picture.

"Thanks, man," Cooper says to him.

"No problem. I'll just be in the background getting some candid shots to surprise you with later."

"Nothing too compromising," Cooper says.

"Don't stifle the artist," Rafael says. "Naked photos are some of my best work."

"Right," I say.

Rafael grins and gives my arm a squeeze. "Congrats again." He walks away, but I'm sure his telephoto lens will still capture us.

A woman with long light brown hair smiles at us. Her hazel eyes sparkle with good humor. "I didn't know I walked into an engagement party."

"It's okay, May," Cooper says. "Still open to the public. What can I get you?"

"Points for the right name," she says. "A glass of merlot, please."

I shoot Cooper a look. I don't want him working on our special day. He inclines his head, understanding. He pours the merlot and gives it to her.

"Last one, I promise," he says to me.

His cousin Mason shows up and claps Cooper on the shoulder. "What're you doing working behind the bar? Get out here. I'll do that."

Mason goes behind the bar and gives May a sexy smile. She stares at him for a moment before exclaiming, "I know you! You're that guy on *Hot Finds*. I love that show."

Cooper joins me, kissing my temple. He's so affectionate and wonderful.

Mason leans an elbow on the bar, getting close to May. "That's me. Cool that you watch the show. We have mostly a male demographic."

"You're even more good looking in person." She slaps a hand over her mouth. "I can't believe I said that out loud."

"Say whatever you want. I love to hear it. I'm Mason."

"I know." She laughs. "I'm May O'Hare. My grandparents used to own this place. Back then it was called Garner's Sports Bar & Grill."

"Is that right? Well, I'm glad you walked in today, May."

"Me too."

Cooper and I exchange a look. Seems like a love connection in the making as Mason and May gaze into each other's eyes.

"Lot of *M* names in my family," Mason says. "My three

younger brothers have names that start with an *M*, two of my cousins, and my mom."

"And now you met another *M*, me."

"May, you're the prettiest one of them all."

"I hope so if you're comparing me to your brothers!"

They laugh.

"Mommy! Mommy!" A little girl around five years old with her brown hair in pigtails runs up to May.

May stands and picks her up. "Did you have fun at the bookstore?"

I do a double take as a woman who looks exactly like May joins her. Identical twins. "Sorry. I kept her distracted as long as I could."

Mason stares at the little girl and then at May.

"Single mom," May says.

Mason shifts uncomfortably.

"Mommy, that's Mason from *Hot Finds*!" the little girl exclaims. "Can I get your autograph?"

"Come on," Cooper says to me. "I want to slow dance with my new fiancée."

I follow him. "But there's no music."

"Back room," he says, taking my hand and guiding me to the empty back room. He goes to the jukebox and plays an upbeat song, "Happy Together."

He twirls me around and brings me close. "This song reminds me of us. Happy once we got together."

I twirl away. "You were already happy."

He takes both my hands in his. "Never as much as when I fell for you. I love you so much."

"I love you too so much."

And then we dance like no one's watching. A joyful dance of two people meant for each other. I laugh as Mackenzie and Harper join us, then Hailey and Josh. Within moments, the whole family's dancing with us.

Rafael whistles loudly. "Rowan, Cooper, over here!"

We turn to the camera, and he takes our picture, in love surrounded by family. It's a dream come true to finally be part of a big loving family. Cooper's a dream come true too. I finally found where I belong.

Cooper frames my face in his hands and kisses me tenderly. This man is beyond my wildest fantasies. I'm the luckiest woman in the world.

He whispers in my ear, "I'm the luckiest man in the world."

I laugh. "I was just thinking I was the luckiest woman in the world."

"See? A perfect match."

Love showed up when I least expected it. Completely inconvenient, yet completely right.

Don't miss the next book in the series, *The Sweet Part*, featuring single mom, May, who's about to open a B&B with some help from Mason. But is Mason ready for an instant family?

Sign up for my newsletter to be emailed when *The Sweet Part* releases. https://www.kyliegilmore.com/newsletter

P.S. Check out Cooper's parents and their legendary frenemy war in the book *Hidden Hollywood.*

Not My Romeo (Book 6)

Rev Me Up (Book 7)

An Ambitious Engagement (Book 8)

Clutch Player (Book 9)

A Tempting Friendship (Book 10)

Clover Park Bride: Nico and Lily's Wedding

A Valentine's Day Gift (Book 11)

Maggie Meets Her Match (Book 12)

The Clover Park Charmers series <<sweet and sexy charmers!

Almost Over It (Book 1)

Almost Married (Book 2)

Almost Fate (Book 3)

Almost in Love (Book 4)

Almost Romance (Book 5)

Almost Hitched (Book 6)

The Rourkes Series <<swoonworthy princes and kickass princesses!

Royal Catch (Book 1)

Royal Hottie (Book 2)

Royal Darling (Book 3)

Royal Charmer (Book 4)

Royal Player (Book 5)

Royal Shark (Book 6)

Rogue Prince (Book 7)

Rogue Gentleman (Book 8)

Rogue Rascal (Book 9)

Rogue Angel (Book 10)

Rogue Devil (Book 11)

Rogue Beast (Book 12)

Unleashed Romance <<steamy romcoms with dogs!

Fetching (Book 1)

Dashing (Book 2)

Sporting (Book 3)

Toying (Book 4)

Blazing (Book 5)

Chasing (Book 6)

Daring (Book 7)

Leading (Book 8)

Racing (Book 9)

Loving (Book 10)

**Check out my website for the most up-to-date list of my books:
kyliegilmore.com/books**

ABOUT THE AUTHOR

Kylie Gilmore is the *USA Today* bestselling author of over fifty humorous contemporary romances. Her series include Happy Endings in Clover Park, Unleashed Romance, the Rourkes, the Happy Endings Book Club, Clover Park, and Clover Park Charmers. With more than three million downloads of her books, readers all over the world love escaping into her hilarious feel-good romances featuring strong bonds with family, friends, and community.

Kylie lives in New York with her family. When she's not writing, reading hot romance, or dutifully taking notes at writing conferences, you can find her happily crafting what will surely be future family heirlooms.

Sign up for Kylie's Newsletter and get a FREE book! kyliegilmore.com/newsletter

For text alerts on Kylie's new releases, text KYLIE to the number (888) 707-3025. (US only)

For more fun stuff check out Kylie's website https://www.kyliegilmore.com.